The Pe

Do I Have Good Luck with Guys or What? ...Nope!

K.R. Denson

DEDICATION

This book is dedicated to my lovely children, Niko & Jade
Denson.
May you both find peace, true love and happiness!

CONTENTS

ACKNOWLEDGMENTS

Editing by Kate Studer
Cover art by Caitlin B. Alexander

1 THE FROWN AND THE POPULAR FLIRT

It was the first day of school and Pamela was in the third grade. She was so excited to see her friends.

"I hope all my friends are in my class!" Pamela said to her dad, Lee, over video chat.

"I hope you have a great day, sweetie. I must get to work now. I love you," Lee said.

"I love you, too!" Pamela said as she waved goodbye. Her mom, Sarah, turned the tablet off and placed it back on the table.

"I wish Dad didn't have to live so far away," Pamela said with a sigh.

"I know, but Marines have a very important job to do, and he will come to visit you as soon as he can. He is always thinking of you and loves you very much," Sarah said lovingly.

"Now, let's get going, hun. We don't want to be late to sign you up for the after-school program," Sarah said.

They arrived at the school and walked through the hallways toward the gymnasium. As they made their way through, Pamela saw her best friend, Jessica.

"Hey, Jessica!" Pamela said.

"Hey, Pamela! I hope we're in the same class!" exclaimed Jessica. Pamela and her mom kept walking in a hurry.

"She is such a sweet girl. I am glad that you have nice friends," Sarah said.

They continued to walk through the halls and Pamela saw her first crush, Rod, walking into one of the classrooms. She'd had a crush on him since they first met the year before. He'd been the new kid in school, and at the time, Pamela had been too shy to talk to him or play with him during recess.

"Hey, Rod!" Pamela yelled as she waved to him. She blushed a little.

Rod waved back to Pamela and then walked inside the classroom.

"Who is that young man?" Sarah asked Pamela with a smirk.

"Just a boy who was in my class last year," Pamela said.

Pamela clearly had a crush on him and Sarah found it adorable that Pamela was trying to hide her excitement over seeing him.

They made it to the gym where the sign-up tables were. They walked up to the woman at the table. "Hi! I need to sign my daughter up for the after-school program," Sarah said.

"What is your daughter's name?" the woman asked.

"Pamela Ann Jones," Sarah said.

The woman scanned through the papers she had under her clipboard. "I'm sorry, I do not see your daughter's name on the list of registered students for this school," the woman said.

"That doesn't make any sense. My daughter has been attending this school for years," Sarah said. Pamela was starting to feel nervous; she did not understand what was going on.

The woman said, "I am sorry, but it seems that your daughter is no longer zoned for this school. She is now zoned for Williamson Elementary School."

Pamela's mom said, "This is ridiculous. Why couldn't someone have called to notify me before I brought my daughter here?! Let's go, Pamela."

Pamela was crushed. Not only did she have to leave all her friends behind, but she had to leave Rod behind too! As the tears ran down her face, she and her mom walked back to the car. "Why are we leaving, Mom? Why can't I go to this school anymore?" Pamela asked.

"They changed the rules and now you have to go to the other school. I'm so sorry, my love." They got into the car and headed to her new school, the tears still pouring down Pamela's face. She was devastated and nervous. Not only was it the first day of school, but now she would be late and would have to make new friends. *Will they even like me?* Pamela wondered.

They arrived at Williamson Elementary School. "You'll be alright, hun. You will make friends fast. I love you," Sarah said to her daughter.

"I love you too, Mom," Pamela said with tears still dripping down her face. Sarah walked Pamela to the classroom and spoke with the teacher, Mrs. Jenna, telling her the situation. Pamela walked into the new classroom and was greeted with a warm smile from the teacher and her new classmates.

"Everyone, this is Pamela. She just transferred here from Bentley Elementary school. Please be kind to her because this has been a hard day for her so far," said Mrs. Jenna.

Mrs. Jenna told Pamela to find an empty seat. Pamela walked over to a seat that was in the back corner.

"Hi, my name is Mya!" the girl next to Pamela said.

"Hi, Mya," Pamela greeted her while grabbing a toy.

Another girl walked up to Pamela and said, "Hey, I'm Lisa. Are you okay?"

"Hi, Lisa. I'm sad because I had to leave all my friends at my other school," Pamela said.

"We will be your friends!" said the two girls. Pamela was starting to feel better and did not feel so alone.

A year went by, and Mya and Lisa became Pamela's best friends. She was happy at her new school, adjusting very well, and she even had her eyes on a new boy in the class!

"Nick is so cute!" Pamela said to Lisa.

"Everyone likes him," said Lisa.

Pamela thought to herself, *He doesn't like me; he likes those other girls*. Pamela was a good, quiet girl. The boys did not seem to like her. *Why can't a cute boy like me?* she wondered.

"Don't worry about him," Lisa told Pamela. "He's trouble. He flirts with all the girls."

The next week, Pamela invited Lisa to sleep over.

"What do you want to do?" Pamela asked Lisa.

"Let's watch music videos and try to copy the dances!" said Lisa.

"That sounds fun! Maybe if I show Nick one of the dances, he will like me?" Pamela suggested hopefully.

Lisa rolled her eyes and said, "Pamela, I told you. He's not a good boy and I don't think you should like him anymore."

"Maybe you're right," said Pamela with a slight frown. They continued playing the same music video over and over and over, trying to learn all the moves.

"I'm getting tired. Let's go to bed," said Lisa.

"Okay," said Pamela. But she did not want to go to sleep just yet. Pamela stayed up, wondering what Nick was doing. Was he asleep or was he awake, too? *I wonder why he doesn't like me? Why doesn't he give me valentines or flirt with me? I guess he doesn't think I am cute or maybe it is because I don't dress like the other girls he flirts with. I wonder if he knows that I like him? Maybe I should show him somehow?* Pamela had made up her mind. She was going to muster the courage to talk to Nick when she went back to school! *Okay, I won't be shy. I will talk to him, so he knows I like him.*

The next day, Pamela and Lisa played outside.

"Hey y'all!" a girl yelled from the other apartment building. Pamela and Lisa looked up and saw that it was Mya.

"Hey!" both girls replied.

"Hey Pamela, come over here. I have to tell you

something!" Mya yelled. Lisa went back inside to get ready to get picked up by her mom after lunch and Pamela raced over to see what Mya wanted to tell her. "Nick told me to tell you that he thinks you're cute," Mya secretly told Pamela while they played on the white bicycle bars. Pamela lit up with excitement.

"Really!? But he doesn't flirt with me at school," Pamela said with a curious look on her face.

"He told me he likes you. And guess what? He moved in next door today." Pamela started getting butterflies in her belly. "I have to go and eat lunch but come back outside and he will come out too. I'll see you tomorrow," Mya said.

"Okay," said Pamela, then she went back in to eat lunch with Lisa before she went home.

Lisa's mom arrived and picked her up after lunch. "Bye y'all and thank you," said Lisa.

"Bye," said Pamela. "Mom, I'm gonna go back outside to play."

"Okay, hun, but remember to stay in front of the building, so I can see you." Pamela went outside to hang on the bicycle bars in front of her apartment building. *I wonder if he is home right now?* Pamela thought. She walked over to the green electrical box that was the midpoint between the two buildings. She sat there, kicking her feet on the box, wondering what she would tell him when they talked for the first time.

Pamela saw some movement from the porch

window. *Is that him!?* she wondered. Maybe he still could not see her. She decided to move closer to the other building and play on the white bicycle bars.

"Psssst! Psssst!" Pamela heard from the window. She looked up with a smile and waved to the person. *OMG it is really him! I hope he is coming down to play!* Pamela thought. She patiently waited and played on the bike bars for about an hour. She was wondering why he did not want to come play. He saw her down there and saw her wave. Pamela knew she could not wait any longer. She had to go back inside. *Now he's gonna think that I don't like him anymore!* Pamela was thinking. She frowned as she headed back inside.

The next day, Pamela went back outside, hoping to see Nick. She walked towards the front of the apartment and sat on the hard, concrete steps to see if anyone was outside playing. She saw cars leaving and entering the complex. She saw a few kids come out and play, but still no sign of Nick. Had Mya lied? Was this just a joke? Pamela did not want to give up hope, so she stayed outside and moved closer to the other building, just as she had the day before. *Maybe he will see me today*, she thought. She played on the bike bars again, flipping around on them and hanging from them, hoping to impress Nick, if he was watching her.

"Hey Pamela," said a boy's voice. Pamela started getting butterflies in her tummy again. She looked up and didn't see anyone. *That sounded like Nick! Maybe Mya was telling the truth!* Pamela thought with excitement.

"Come up here. I have a surprise for you," The boy's voice said. Pamela got off the bike bars and dusted herself off. She wanted to make sure she looked okay. She glanced at the top of the concrete stairs and it really was him!

Her voice was crackly as she said, "Hey Nick. What's the surprise?"

Nick told her to come up to see. She slowly walked up the stairs while her heart was beating so fast! She made it to the top and there he was, standing with the front door open.

As Pamela stood there, Nick pushed the door open more. Pamela stayed where she was. She looked in and saw a lit tea candle on the porch railing. "That's so pretty!" Pamela said.

Nick looked at her with a twinkle in his eyes and told her, "That's for you. Wanna come play?"

RED FLAG. Pamela started thinking, *This is not a good idea. I don't think his parents are home. I don't wanna get in trouble*. Pamela asked Nick, "Are your parents home?"

Nick replied, "Nope, they are at work, but my big sister is here. Are you gonna come in?"

Pamela responded, "No thank you. I'm not allowed to come in without your parents home."

Nick walked over to the balcony, took the

candle down and blew the flame out. "Okay. Bye then," he said.

Pamela walked down the stairs as if everything was okay, but inside, she was sad again. She really liked him, but she did not want to break the rules.

"Did you have fun outside today?" Sarah asked Pamela.

"Yeah, Mom. I saw a friend from school who just moved here," Pamela replied.

"That's good, hun," her mom said. "Now, go get ready for dinner."

Pamela was so sad. She had gotten so close to Nick and was sad that she could not play with him that day. *It's not fair. It's hard being the good girl and following the rules*, she thought. After dinner, Pamela went to take a shower and get ready for bed. She walked into her room and could not go to sleep. *Maybe he does like me, and he was just trying to be nice?* she thought. She did not think that he would do that for other girls. Maybe he just did that for her because he thought she was special? That thought made her smile again. "I can't wait to see him in school tomorrow!"

Sarah walked into the room and hugged Pamela. "Good night, hun. I love you," said her mom.

"I love you, too, Mom." Pamela rushed to sleep, so tomorrow would come faster.

The next morning, Pamela scarfed down her

breakfast in a hurry to get to school. Her mom looked at her and wondered why she was in such a hurry. They both finished breakfast and then Sarah drove Pamela to school. Pamela walked into class and saw Nick. He smiled at her and she smiled back. *Yay, he still likes me!* she thought. *Maybe he will play with me during playtime?* She was getting anxious and could not concentrate on her schoolwork. It seemed like time was going by so slowly. After refocusing on her work, playtime finally came around. Pamela walked over to the blocks and started to build something. She did not like blocks, but she knew he liked playing with them. A few minutes went by and Nick was not around.

Where is he? He loves playing with blocks. Pamela stood up and walked around to see where he was playing.

"He He Tee He Heee!" She heard giggling in the corner of the classroom, where the play mats were. It looked like someone had built a fort! Pamela inched closer to see who was playing in the fort. She peeked in and saw Nick playing with another girl! Pamela's heart sank. *He really doesn't like me!* she thought. She felt jealous and hurt at the same time and did not know what to do. She went to go play with Lisa and told her what happened.

"It's okay, friend," Lisa said to Pamela, but Pamela frowned and pouted all day.

It was time for everyone to get ready to go home. All the kids went outside to play, while they waited. Pamela walked around the play yard and caught

a glimpse of Nick. *Maybe he doesn't like that girl?*
Maybe they were just playing together as friends? she
thought. She saw her mom pull up in the parking lot.
She raced over to Nick to try to say goodbye to him, to
show him that she was not mad at him for playing with
that other girl.

FLOP! Oh no! Pamela tripped on herself and
skinned her knee! She quickly stood up and waved to
Nick with an awkward, painful smile and then ran to the
teacher. She didn't want to show Nick that she was hurt
and embarrassed for falling in front him.

She cried and said, "I fell and skinned my knee!"

Mrs. Jenna hugged her and cleaned her wound.
"You'll be okay, sweetie. There's your mom." Pamela
thanked her and went to the car.

"Are you okay, hun?" Sarah asked after kissing
Pamela's knee. Pamela shook her head, no, and told her
mom about what happened that day.

2 THE FROWN AND THE MYSTERY CRUSH AT THE COMPLEX

A few months after her experiences with Nick, Pamela finally returned to normal. When she went to school, she simply pretended that Nick was not there, and she no longer felt sad. When she played outside at home, she played with her friends from school who had just moved in next door. It was great! They played board games, played in the pool, and went exploring in the woods behind their building every day. Pamela was having so much fun, she was not thinking about boys at all—until she saw HIM.

It was finally the weekend again and Pamela wanted to play outside, but her friends were out of town. She walked outside and sat on the concrete stairs to get some fresh air and people watch. Out of nowhere, she saw a boy pushing a scooter across the sidewalk by the metal mail boxes. He was slim, tall, wore basketball shorts and a t-shirt with a red cap. He smiled at her! Pamela thought, *He is so cute! Is he smiling at me!? Who is this boy? I've never seen him here before!* Pamela smiled back and he just kept on zooming across the sidewalk over and over. They were both too shy to approach each other. After a while, he asked her to come talk to him across the street.

Pamela replied, "I can't. I have to stay in front of the building."

He shouted, "My name is Sean. What's your name?"

Pamela smiled and shouted back, "My name is Pamela!"

"Sean! Time to come in!" a woman's voice called. Both of their smiles turned into frowns.

"I have to go!" Sean shouted.

"Okay," Pamela shouted back, still frowning. *I finally found a boy who likes me, and I may never see him again!* Pamela was very distraught and was feeling sad again. He did not go to her school, she did not know whether he was visiting someone in the apartment complex, or if he lived there. She had never seen him before, so most likely, he did not live there. *Maybe I can still see him again,* she thought. *If I hang out on the stairs every day, I might!* She felt slightly hopeful. This was meant to be!

Days went by with no sign of the cute boy in the red cap. Pamela continued to play on the stairs daily and she was always on the lookout for the color red. If her friends wanted to go to the park or the pool, she would go, but for only a short while. She did not want to be gone too long just in case he showed up. Now, days had turned into weeks.

Aw man...I really may never see him again! Pamela thought to herself. She was so saddened by the thought of it, but she never gave up. She continued playing and waiting, playing, and waiting. This connection was magical. She felt as if she was a princess and this was her prince charming. She was willing to hold on to this dream no matter how long it took!

A year went by and still no visit from the cute boy in the red cap. But, by then, Pamela was pre-occupied with thoughts of the cute twins from upstairs! They had taken her mind right off Sean! The new family had moved upstairs a month ago. The mom went to work daily, the dad worked from home, and all three brothers went to high school. Yes, Pamela had upgraded to older boys. They were all cute, but the twins were SO cute!! Pamela had always been able to tell the difference between twins and this time was no different.

She zeroed in on the quiet twin. His name was Jason. She did not realize it, but she liked how mysterious he was. That mystery gave her the same feelings that Sean had given her. She started hanging out on the concrete stairs, as usual, but for a different purpose this time. She knew that every time Jason left the house, he would HAVE to come down the stairs. That was her excuse to see him every day and maybe hint to him that she liked him.

One day, Jason came out to hang on the stairs. He pulled out a cigarette that smelled like vanilla and started smoking it.

Pamela asked him, "Why are you doing that? Isn't that bad for you?".

He smirked and replied, "Well, it is not good for you, but I like doing it."

RED FLAG. Pamela started thinking, *I don't like that he smokes. That is not good. But he is SO cute! Maybe if I show him that it does not bother me, then maybe he will like me?* Here she went again, ignoring red flags. She totally did not acknowledge that he was too old for her and could get in trouble for liking her, but she was also putting herself in a bad situation. Secondhand smoke was not safe, even if it was outside. But Pamela continued to hang out by the stairs and tried to avoid the path of the smoke.

Okay, this isn't working, Pamela thought to herself. *He's not flirting with me at all. Why doesn't he like me? We see each other almost every day.* She was a little sad, but she was happy that she at least got to see a cute boy every day. She would have tried to hang out with the other twin, DJ, but he always kept to himself inside.

"Who's that over there?" Jason asked Pamela.

"Who?" Pamela responded.

"That guy over there, wearing a red cap," said Jason.

Pamela's eyes lit up and it felt like she had piranhas in her belly! *Could that be Sean!? No way, that's impossible...it's been so long!* Pamela thought to herself.

The guy waved and started coming over to Pamela and Jason. "OMG is that really him!?" Pamela muttered under her breath. As he made his way across the street, Pamela started to realize that it *was* him!

Since Jason was done smoking, he headed back upstairs. Pamela waved goodbye to him, but quickly put her focus back on Sean.

As Sean got closer, she ran up to him and gave him a gentle hug. She did not want to look like she had been thinking of him all this time. She wanted to see if he still really liked her or if he was just being friendly.

Sean told Pamela, "Hey, it's been a long time. My cousin, who lived here, moved, so my mom never brought me back."

"It's okay," Pamela said to him. "I just can't believe you're back. I thought I'd never see you again."

Both walked over to the green electrical box to talk.

"What's your name again?" Sean finally asked her.

"It's Pamela. And you are Sean, right?"

"Yeah, Sean. Sean Wrotten," he told her. "Don't pick on me about my last name, please. A lot of people do that."

"Why would I pick on your name?" Pamela asked innocently.

"Because it sounds like rotten," he said.

"I like your name!" Pamela said kindly to him. "At least I will never forget your name, since it is so unique."

Sean smiled and said, "Thanks."

Pamela began writing his name on the ground in chalk. "Is this how you spell your name?" she asked.

"Yup, that's right! People usually spell it wrong," he replied.

Score! Pamela thought to herself. There is no way he does not like her now. She got his name right! *Yes!*

"If your cousin moved away, why are you here?" Pamela asked Sean.

"I have a friend who lives out here now and my mom dropped me off to visit him." Pamela was excited to hear this news. Maybe now she would be able to see him more often! The two began asking each other several questions to get to know each other better. "What's your favorite color?" "What's your favorite show?" "What's your favorite song?" The questions just kept coming from them both. *This guy definitely likes me likes me!* Pamela thought. *He is really trying to get to know me.*

18

"Where do you live, Sean?" she asked him.

"I live, like, an hour away from here, in a place called Newberry."

"Oh, okay. That is so far away," said Pamela, frowning slightly.

"My dad is trying to get a new job here, so I might live here soon!" Sean said. That was music to her ears. She felt like her fairy tale was closer to coming true!

"We have to go!" said a woman's voice from across the street.

"That's my mom. I have to go," Sean said sadly.

"Okay, I hope I get to see you again. I am going to miss you!" said Pamela.

"I'm going to miss you, too," he said. They quickly gave each other their cell phone numbers, online chatroom screen names, and a hug and then he was gone...AGAIN. *I have lost him again! Who knows if his dad will get the new job!* Pamela was so sad. The chance of seeing him again was already slim, but now it felt impossible!

Once again, she got into her routine of hanging out at the stairs, waiting to see if Sean would show up. Always searching for the red cap. Jason would occasionally hang out by the stairs, but she did not care anymore. Seeing Sean again made her realize that she needed to give her attention to someone her own age.

Jason now felt like just a friend to her and Pamela started to try to get advice from him instead.

Pamela asked him, "Do you think that guy really likes me? How do I know if he really does?"

Jason replied, "Well, does he seem happy when he sees you? Does he like talking to you? Does he have fun when you are together?"

"Yeah," she said.

"Then I think he really likes you. It is hard, because he lives far away, and you guys can't hang out with each other. You two are young and should try to move on. You'll find another boy out there."

Another year went by and Pamela had not seen or heard from Sean. She never contacted him, because she wanted to see if he truly was interested in her and liked her. *I guess his dad didn't' get the job,* she thought to herself. She decided to just let it go. She was tired of torturing herself, dreaming of them being together. It was time to move on. New school, fresh start. She was now going into the sixth grade. Middle School! Pamela was not worried about going to a new school this time. Most of her friends were going to the same school anyway, so it should be fun! The new school was called Bishop Ward Middle School. It had brick walls and lots of grass. The classes were a lot of fun and she had at least one friend in each!

The school day was over, and it was time for Pamela to walk home with her friends. The great thing about walking home was that a lot of other kids were walking home too, and all towards the same neighborhood. Never a boring moment after school! While leaving the school, Pamela saw a cute guy hanging around on the corner. *Here we go again...*

3 THE FROWN AND THE BAD BOY WITH POTENTIAL

"Hey wassup?" the guy said to Pamela.

"They exchanged names. His name was Chase. He looked older and clearly did not go to middle school. So, Pamela asked him how old he was.

He said, "I'm a couple years older than you."

RED FLAG. Pamela started thinking, *an older guy is talking to me! He must think I'm really pretty!* So, she decided to play hard to get and kept on walking with her friends. She did not want to seem like a desperate younger girl, getting excited about an older guy talking to her.

Her friends giggled and asked, "Why didn't you want to keep talking to him!?"

Pamela giggled too, and said, "I want to see if he will be back tomorrow and if he is, I will talk to him a little more then!"

All night, Pamela had dreamt of the new guy at the corner. She wondered how old he really was. Was he a creep or a good guy? What was he doing there anyway? So many questions. She could hardly sleep that night. She was tossing and turning and trying so hard not to think of him. How could she have a crush on someone the first time she saw them? Maybe it was love at first sight. The thought of him made her lightheaded, with butterflies in her stomach. *Okay, if I see him tomorrow, I have to act cool and not show him how excited I am to see him,* Pamela thought. She hoped that he would not see through her and think she was just a little girl.

The next morning, Pamela jumped out of bed and began to get ready for breakfast. She did not want her mom to know about this new guy yet, so she tried to hide her excitement. She just ate her food at a normal pace and tried to keep from smiling more than usual. "Hey, hun, why are you so giddy this morning?" Sarah asked Pamela. Of course, Sarah saw right through Pamela's act.

"No reason. Why are you asking me that?" Pamela replied.

"I know you; I can see it on your face...it's a boy, isn't it?" her mom said with a smirk.

Pamela started to blush and looked down with a matching smirk. "Yes, Mom...it's a new boy I met yesterday at school. He was there on the corner when school was let out and he said hi to us."

Sarah looked puzzled. "Was he already standing at the corner when you guys got to that spot? Does he go to your school?" Sarah asked Pamela.

Pamela replied innocently, "He was already there. I don't know, Mom. I think he goes to our school, but he looks older than us."

Sarah looked concerned and said, "Hun, be careful. Remember that even though he seems nice and you think he is cute; he is still a stranger. Don't go anywhere with him and stay with your friends while you walk home. Promise me."

"Okay, Mom, I promise I will be careful." Pamela said sweetly. Pamela was wondering what all the fuss was about, but listened to her mom as she always did, no matter what.

Pamela knocked on her neighbors' door to see if her friends were ready to walk to school. She was in a hurry to get to school, so that the day would go by faster, and she could see him again! *Hopefully, he will be there again. I don't want to get my heart broken again like with Sean,* she thought, followed by a long sigh.

Her friends finally came out and they started heading to school. Of course, the day went super slowly. Pamela was looking at the clock every two minutes, while making paper origami animals. She clearly could not concentrate.

"Pamela....Pamela!" shouted Mr. Spenser.

"Huh? Sorry," said Pamela.

"What is the answer to my question?" Mr. Spencer said sarcastically.

"Ummm...ten?" Pamela guessed unconvincingly.

"Pamela, the question was, what is the fourth planet in our solar system?" Mr. Spencer repeated.

"Oh...it's Mars," Pamela said quickly. Lisa looked at Pamela and smiled then rolled her eyes. She knew why Pamela was distracted. Only a boy would do that to her.

At lunch, everyone started bustling and getting chatty as they got ready to go to the lunchroom.

"Single file line, everyone!" Mr. Spencer shouted. The class lined up and headed to the lunchroom. They were all excited because it was pizza day! Through the food line and to the cafeteria benches everyone went. Pamela, Lisa, Mya, and the whole crew sat together as they usually did. Of course, lunch period could not go any slower for Pamela! You would think she would be distracted with all that went on during that time—all the gossip and passing of handwritten notes—but one thing did catch her eye. Her friend, Kim, was spreading ranch dressing onto her pizza slice.

"Umm...Kim, what are you doing?" Pamela asked.

"I'm putting ranch dressing on my pizza. It is SO good, girl! You should try it!" Kim said, laughing.

Everyone at the table was hesitant but decided to try it. "It's not that bad." "Okay, okay, it is good." "It's okay, I guess." There were mixed feelings about the new taste combination she had come up with.

Then, Pamela said, "Have you guys ever tried applesauce on your pizza?"

Everyone looked at her with disgust. "Ummm...NO!" said Mitch, one of her friends at the table.

"It's so good!" Pamela said with a smile.

Mitch asked her, "What made you want to try that!? Ranch dressing is bad enough!"

Pamela responded, "It was actually a mistake in elementary school. This cute boy accidentally bumped into me in the lunch line and my applesauce spilled onto my pizza. I wanted to show him that it was okay, so I just ate it and I actually liked it!"

Everyone shook their heads and giggled.

"Of course, there was a boy involved," Mya said jokingly.

The lunch bell rang and now it was time to walk back to class.

"Single file line, everyone!" said the principal. He was always hanging out during lunch period and speaking to the kids. They all thought he was cool. As they made their way back to class, Pamela started daydreaming about Chase.

"Pamela! Pamela!" called Lisa.

"What!?" Pamela responded.

"You better not be thinking about that guy," Lisa said, laughing.

"Girl, I can't help it! He's so cute and I still can't believe he talked to me!" Pamela just kept on gushing over this guy. She could not focus for the rest of the day and did not complete her assignments. *Oh, well*, she thought. *He is totally worth it!*

YES!!!!!!!! The end of day announcements came on. It was almost time for school to be out! Pamela could not even focus on what the principle was saying over the intercom and was already all packed up! But ugh! The second hand on the clock would NOT move! *5...4...3...2...1...RING! RING! RING!*

Yes! Pamela jumped up and ran out of the door. *Crap, I have to meet my friends first, so we can walk home!* Pamela had to slow her roll and remember what her mom said.

"Hey Pamela, over here!" her friends called. Pamela ran over to them and they all started walking past the schoolyard and onto the city sidewalk. As she was walking, she was trying not to look obvious. She was clearly searching for him but didn't want anyone to notice.

She looked over and there he was! *Yes!* She tried SO hard not to smile too big, but he was smiling big too! As Pamela and her friends got closer to the corner, he started walking towards them.

"Hey, Pamela," Chase said.

"Hey Chase, what are you doing here again today?" she asked.

"I'm here waiting for my little brother, Daniel," he said.

"Oh okay. Do you go to this school, too? I never see you there." Pamela said.

"I was supposed to start going to Southside High School, but since I work to help my mom out, I can't be in school right now," Chase admitted.

"Oh okay," replied Pamela. She was an incredibly open person, even at this age. She didn't care that he wasn't in school. That just made him more interesting to her.

"Here," Chase said, handing her a note.

"What's this?" Pamela asked, looking at him with twinkling eyes.

"It's for you. Read it later and write me back," he said with a smile.

"Okay, I will. Bye!"

The group continued walking home and Pamela was walking on air with her head in the clouds! She seemed unbothered by her friends trying to tease her about how she was acing. "Look at Pamela y'all. She's all in love!" "Pamela, let us read the letter!" "Read it now!" Pamela wanted to read it but did not want to betray Chase's trust by not keeping it private.

"No!" Pamela said jokingly. Everyone arrived at the complex and continued to giggle and playfully taunt Pamela.

"Bye y'all!" she yelled and ran right home. She was in such a rush to read the letter that she forgot to say hi to her mom. She threw her backpack on her bed and pulled out the letter.

"What is this?" Pamela said to herself. As she looked down at the letter, all she saw were symbols. She looked back up towards the top of the letter and saw the code legend.

There were three tic-tac-toe games on the paper, but with all the letters of the alphabet on them. There were also dots on them. The first game had the letters A-I and had no dot over the game. The next game had the letters J-R in them and there was one dot over that game. The final game had letters S-Z in them with two dots over that game. Pamela looked down at the first symbol and started thinking, *Okay, there are lines that make up a box with the bottom line missing and there is no dot inside of it...* She looked up at the legend. *Okay, that first symbol must be an H!* She moved on to the next symbol. *Okay, this one has two lines...one on the left and one at the top with no dot.* She looked at the legend and saw the I inside that shape. "HI!" she said out loud. She was so excited that she was figuring out the letters! She needed to find a pencil or something, so she could continue.

She zoomed across the room to her little desk to find a pencil. Of course, she could not find one right when she needed it! She opened all the drawers, looked under the desk, looked in her backpack and finally found one deep down in the pocket of the backpack. So, she went ahead and continued deciphering the symbols. The next symbol had two lines—one on the top and one on the right with one dot in it. "That is a P. Okay, the rest of the letters are easy. It's my name," Pamela said. She continued until the translation was complete. The full note read: *Hi Pamela. Wassup? I hope you can read this note. I will see you tomorrow. - Chase*

Pamela did not know what to do with herself!

During dinner, she tried to eat at a normal pace, so her mom would not figure out her excitement. Of course, once again, that did not work.

"Hun, why are you smiling so hard? What happened at school?" Her mom knew it had to be the boy they were talking about yesterday.

"The cool guy I met gave me a note today!"

Sarah looked at Pamela with a smile. "I know you like him, but remember, you still don't know him or know why he hangs out at that corner."

Pamela responded with a grin. "I do know,

actually. He's there to pick up his little brother."

Sarah breathed a sigh of relief. She was happy to know that he was not being a creep and that he was there for a reason, but she still wasn't okay with him. Pamela finished dinner and went right to sleep. She wanted the night to fly by!

Months went by and every week, Pamela and Chase exchanged letters. As they grew closer, their moms decided to allow them to hang out at his family's house one day, so the moms could get to know each other too. Pamela was so excited! This was really getting real! Pamela and her mom arrived at the house in a matter of minutes. *How cool is this? He lives so close!* Pamela thought to herself. The moms introduced themselves and had a long chat in the house, while Pamela and Chase stayed outside. They first had several rounds of competitions to see who could stand on his tall wood stilts the longest.
"One...two...three...four...five...six...seven...ugh!" Pamela shouted. She could not stay on the stilts for long but kept trying. Of course, Chase could stay on them the longest.

Then, he asked, "Hey, do you know how to skateboard?"

Pamela responded, "Yeah! I have one in my mom's car. It's hard finding other people who know how."

Chase taught her a trick and after several tries, she got it! She was having SO much fun! A couple of hours later, their moms walked out of the house, laughing and smiling.

"Okay, Pamela, it's time to go home," Sarah said. Before she left, Chase ran into the house to get her something. He remembered how much she liked those trading cards with all the different characters on them. She mentioned them in her letters often. He had a set and gave them to her! Pamela was so touched, because people paid a lot of money to get these cards and he just gave them to her so easily.

"Thank you so much!" Pamela said. Everyone said goodbye and Sarah and Pamela went home.

"His mom is great, and I like them. He seems extremely sweet, but he seems to get into trouble a lot and he smokes," Sarah said to Pamela. Pamela was unbothered and just smiled and began replaying the visit in her head.

Months went by and Chase had been visiting Pamela at the complex often. They would hang out on the concrete stairs and talk for hours. They would hold hands and hug and talk and talk. Then one day, he leaned in to kiss her!

"Wait! I've never done this before," Pamela said embarrassingly.

"It's okay. Do you want me to teach you?" Chase asked with a grin.

"Yeah, okay," Pamela said. They leaned in for the kiss and Pamela felt awkward. "Your mouth feels big," she said while giggling. Chase started to laugh. "You'll get used to it; you just need a little more practice." Every day after that, they would talk for a little and then end the visit with a kissing session.

"Does my mouth still feel big?" Chase asked Pamela, laughing.

She giggled. "No, not anymore!"

During future visits, Chase started disappearing for a little while during each visit. The first time it happened, Pamela asked, "Where did you go?".

"I just went for a quick walk," he told her. The next time, Pamela followed him and started smelling that familiar sweet vanilla smell. She caught him meeting up with Jason to smoke.

"But you told me you wouldn't smoke anymore!" Pamela said.

"I'm sorry but I'm going to do what I want." Chase admitted to her.

"If you can't stop smoking, then we cannot hang out anymore," Pamela said with a sigh. He stayed there and kept smoking, while Pamela slowly walked away. As Pamela entered the house, Sarah saw her crying.

"What's wrong, hun? Did something happen with Chase?"

Pamela looked up and said, "I caught him smoking with Jason. He knows that I do not like that."

Sarah hugged her and said, "I'm sorry. You will be okay. You shouldn't hang around him if he does that. But don't be too hard on him either. Smoking is a difficult habit to break."

Pamela wiped her tears and let out a huge sigh.

4 THE POKER FACE AND THE SMART FLIRT

Time moved on and suddenly, Pamela was waking up to the first day of high school!

Okay, I really need to focus on my work from now on. This is high school, and I have to leave these boys alone, Pamela thought to herself as she got ready. She said bye to her mom and went to see if the next-door neighbors were ready to catch the bus. She knocked on the door and her friends came out.

"Hey Pamela, are you ready for this!?" they asked.

"Of course! I am super focused, y'all. For real this time!" Pamela laughed. As they approached the bus, her other friends, who were already on the bus, began to playfully taunt her and jokingly ask her if she was ready to meet high school guys.

"Ha ha ha. Very funny, you guys! I'm focusing on my schoolwork from now on!" Pamela exclaimed proudly.

"Yeah right, I bet you can't last one day without talking to a guy! You can't talk to a cute guy at all today!" Lisa challenged.

They arrived at the school and everyone got off the bus. Then they all dispersed into separate areas of the open atrium to find their friends' classrooms. Pamela and Lisa hung out in the hallway of the wing where their classroom was, so they could have first pick of seats next to each other. More friends came over and played card games and chatted about what they expected for the day.

"Hey, can I play one round?" A male voice said from behind the crowd.

"Sure! You can be my partner this time," Pamela said.

"Cool. My name is Donnie. What's your name?" he asked.

"I'm Pamela, it's nice to meet you," she answered.

While playing, Donnie revealed that he and his family just moved into town from Pennsylvania a week prior. Since he didn't know anyone, Pamela and her friends offered to hang out with him.

RING! RING! RING!

The first period bell rang out.

"Okay, Pamela, don't think I forgot about our bet!" Lisa said with a smirk.

"I know, I know," Pamela responded. As they settled in, Pamela could not help but scan the room for hotties. *Whew! No new cute guys in here. I already know most of the people. Today will be fun and I will not lose the bet*, Pamela thought.

Her other classes flew by rather quickly with no new cute guys in sight. Pamela, Lisa, and the crew met up at the cafeteria.

"I told y'all I wasn't going to lose this bet!" Pamela proudly exclaimed. Everyone sighed and rolled their eyes while holding in their laughs. But Ted, one of the guys in the group, could not hold it in and he laughed out loud!

"The day isn't over yet," Mya said.

"Whatever, just watch," Pamela responded with a hopeful smile.

While waiting for the bell to ring, Mya saw Pamela looking around the atrium. "Pamela, what are you doing? Why are you looking around like that?"

Pamela laughed and said, "I'm just looking around and people watching, that's all!"

RING! RING! RING!

The lunch bell rang, and it was time to go to the

next class. Pamela was excited because she knew this would be her favorite class. She loved science! Unfortunately, none of her friends from the crew were in this class with her. Pamela found a seat quickly, with a clear view of the whiteboard, and patiently waited for class to begin. Then, to the left of her, she saw movement from the corner of her eye. She turned to look and OMG there was this cute, new guy! Now she was happy that none of her friends were there to catch her looking at him! She got butterflies in her stomach and became a little lightheaded. She tried SO hard to act normal and pretend that he didn't faze her at all. Class began and she was happy about that, because now she could have a distraction.

"Welcome class. I hope you are all having a good first day so far. Time to put away your cell phones. Look up at the board and review the equation. What is the coefficient for oxygen gas when the following equation is balanced?" Mr. Ford asked. Some people had their heads down while some were working through the problem in their heads. This was her chance to try to impress this guy and show him she wasn't only pretty, but smart too!

Pamela raised her hand. "It is eight," she gently answered, as she made origami swans from her notebook paper. She did not want to sound like an overly confident know it all.

"That is correct. Great job," said Mr. Ford. He put a check mark next to the completed equation and wrote a new one. This time, the new guy answered quickly.

"You are correct, sir," said Mr. Ford. Pamela was becoming flushed. Not only was the new guy cute, but he was smart too!

I have to get over my shyness and just talk to him! What do I have to lose? Pamela thought. So, towards the end of the class, she took her time putting her items back into her backpack. She was waiting for most of the other people to leave the classroom. She did not want them to catch on to her plans and risk another girl doing the same thing and stealing her thunder. Pamela took a deep breath, hoping it would give her courage, and then spoke to him. "Hi, my name is Pamela. What's your name?"

"Axel," he said harshly.

RED FLAG. "Have you always lived around here, or did you move from somewhere else?" she asked him.

"From somewhere else," he said quickly.

"Oh, okay," Pamela replied awkwardly.

As he stood up, Axel glared at Pamela and sharply asked, "Any more questions?"

GINOURMOUS RED FLAG. Pamela tried not to appear stunned by his response and replied, "Nope, I guess not."

What the heck is this guy's problem!? He does not want to be bothered, I guess. Maybe he has been asked questions all day and is tired? Pamela thought. As

39

she looked up, she saw Mya kind of hanging off him like how best pals do. *Wait...how and when did this happen? How did she get so close to him already!? Why was he mean like that with me and not with her?* Pamela just could not understand and wanted to know Mya's secret. Being a friend seemed to work for her, but why not for me? It's not fair! The one time I get the guts to talk to a guy that I think is so fine and he shuts me down in the meanest and rudest way possible! *I am NEVER doing that again. Next time, I will wait for the guy to speak to me first, so I will know if he likes me or not.*

She got up and slowly left the classroom with a fake smile on her face. She was trying so hard to not let him see how he hurt her feelings. A few people were hanging out in the hallway waiting for the next class. *Oh great...I have another class with him. Ugh!* Pamela was not excited about this at all. As they waited for the next bell to ring, Pamela looked to the opposite wall and saw Tonya standing there in a strange position. Was that a ballet pose? Why was she standing like that? Pamela scanned the hallway further and saw Axel right there next to her. *Oh okay...she's trying to impress him too huh?* Pamela thought. She stayed close to them, to see if he was going to take the bait. Nope, he seemed uninterested in her too. That made Pamela feel SLIGHTLY better about herself, knowing that she was not the only one looking foolish.

"Hey Pamela, are you okay? How was class?" Donnie asked as he entered the hallway. He noticed that she looked disappointed. He was a very observant guy.

"It was okay. It was my favorite subject—science," Pamela answered. She didn't want him to know why she wasn't feeling great. Afterall, she didn't really know him that well yet.

"That's good. What's your next class?" he asked.

"It's math," Pamela said. "What's your next class?"

"English, my favorite subject. It looks like it is next to your class," Donnie said.

RING RING RING!

"Okay, have a good class and I'll see you later," Donnie said as he walked into his classroom.

Pamela waved and walked into her classroom.

She got though the next class, which was not too bad, because she loved math. She then tried to find Lisa, so she could tell her what just happened. She did not care that she lost the bet, she just needed to vent to her best friend.

"Hey Lisa, you won't believe what just happened!" Pamela said.

"You lost the bet, didn't you? I know about the new guy. All the girls have been trying to talk to him," Lisa said while laughing.

"Yeah, but forget that. Let me tell you what happened!" Pamela told Lisa the story and Lisa could

41

not believe it.

"I'm sorry, friend, but it'll be okay. At least you know what he is like, and you can leave him alone," Lisa said comfortingly.

"I guess you're right," Pamela replied. She could not wait to shake her feelings for this guy.

A few weeks went by and Pamela was doing well. She still had feelings for Axel, but they were no longer consuming her. As she walked into math class, she saw some people crowding a sheet of paper that was posted on the wall, next to the whiteboard.

"What's that?" Pamela asked.

Mya turned around and said, "It's the list for the group project we had to get permission slips signed for. Mr. Cave put us into groups already."

Pamela walked up to the list and read off the names in her head—*Stacey, Pamela, Jeff, and Axel.* She had the butterflies in her stomach again. *Uh oh! Now we have to spend time together! He will have to start liking me after this. There is no way that this group project won't bring us closer together!*

"Everyone, grab your stuff. We're heading to the public library, so you guys can do your research. There are more resources there than we have here, for this project," Mr. Cave announced. Mr. Cave guided everyone out of the classroom, and they all walked to the bus.

"Where's Axel, Mya, and Steve?" someone asked.

"Axel has his own car, so he's driving them there," Mr. Cave explained. Pamela was happy that he would not be riding on the bus and that she had time to prepare herself for working with him. She had to act cool and not show him that her feelings had come back.

They arrived at the library and split into their groups. Pamela anxiously walked up to her group and said, "Okay, let's knock this out." Over the next couple of hours, each group completed their research on harnessing the sun's heat, calculating curves, and were ready to get back to school to build their hot dog cookers.

Everyone gathered their belongings and walked out. Axel, Mya, and Steve walked to the car, while everyone else walked back to the school bus.

Once everyone arrived back to school, they rushed back to the classroom. "Whichever team can get their hotdog to reach the correct temperature first, wins. That means that you have calculated the curve correctly. You have one hour to build your cookers," Mr. Cave said.

Mr. Cave set the timer, and everyone started building. Pamela thought that it would be hard for her to focus while working with Axel, but it was easy enough for her to put her feelings aside. She loved a good contest and this competition was a decent distraction. They made a good team!

One by one, each group got close, but no one reached the correct temperature. *Well, at least we all failed together. I didn't get to impress Axel, but at least we bonded through being on a losing team together,* Pamela thought. Mr. Cave congratulated everyone on their good work and gave prizes to everyone for their efforts. It was now time to go home. Some kids left the school on the bus and some kids were picked up by their parents. Since Axel had a car, he invited the group to go get some fast food before going home. Two of their groupmates declined the ride and decided to meet there instead. Pamela's mom pulled up and Pamela started walking towards the car.

"Hey Pamela, do you want to ride with me to get some food? We're going to meet the others," Axel said. Pamela held up one finger, gesturing for him to hold on while she went to ask her mom.

"Hey Ma, my classmate, Axel, invited me to ride with him to get some food. We are going to meet our other classmates there. Is that okay?"

Sarah hesitated, then said, "Yes, you can, but make sure he drives safely, and you call me as soon as you get there."

Pamela had a huge smile and nodded her head. She composed herself and walked back to Axel's car. "My mom said it was okay, so I can ride with you."

Axel opened her door and Pamela hopped in. Axel jumped in and started the engine. He turned up the music and tried to adjust the volume. Pamela was so shy and did not know what to talk about. Axel put the car in gear and slowly backed up. BANG! Axel stopped the car abruptly and Pamela looked around to see what happened.

They both jumped out of the car and were stunned at the sight. Axel had run into Sarah's car! Pamela called out, "Ma, are you okay?!"

Sarah responded, "Yes, hun. I'm okay." They all crowded the front of her car to inspect the damage. "Looks like the bumper is scratched and the headlight is broken," Sarah said.

Axel paced back and forth with his hands folded above his head yelling, "I am SO sorry! I am SO sorry!"

Pamela's mom replied, "It is okay. We are all okay and that's all that matters. Did you both not hear me? I was honking at you, so you would stop."

"No, I didn't hear it, Ma," said Pamela. Clearly Axel's music had been too loud. Pamela's mom already knew how bad Axel felt and did not want him to feel worse, so she let him go and still allowed the two of them to go get some food.

"This isn't my car; this is my big brother's car. If he sees the scratches, I'm going to be in huge trouble!"

Pamela sighed and said, "Don't worry. My mom is nice. She will just let it go."

After sitting in the car for a few moments to recoup, they finally headed to the fast-food restaurant.

The group met at the booth near the window and Axel told them what just happened.

"OMG Pamela, is your mom okay? What is she going to do?" Mya asked.

"She's okay and won't do anything. She's really nice." Pamela said reassuringly.

While the others continued chatting about the situation, Pamela grew silent. She was thinking, *This could be a good thing! Now we have had a bonding moment. There is no way he does not like me now.*

Kevin looked at Axel and asked, "Bro, are you going to pay to get her mom's car and your brother's car fixed?"

Axel quickly said, "Nope! Her mom said it was okay and I am going to try to hide the scratches on my brother's car!"

Pamela gave Axel the side eye. *Wow*, she thought. *This guy won't even offer to pay for my mom's car light. He is not the guy I thought he was.* Pamela realized that she was stuck in the friend-zone with this guy and you know what? She was okay with that. He was not THAT fine.

5 THE POKER FACE AND THE PRETTY EYED CRUSH

Months flew by and the buzz of the accident had long died down along with Pamela's feelings towards Axel.

"Okay, class. Settle down. We have a new student with us today," Mr. Williams, the history teacher, said. All the students started whispering and looking around to spot the new kid. The new kid was incredibly quiet. "Can you come up and introduce yourself to the class, sir?" Mr. Williams asked him.

The new kid walked up and introduced himself, "Hi, my name is Brian and I just moved here from New York."

"Hi Brian," some of the other students murmured in unison. Brian quietly walked back to his desk and sat down. Mr. Williams turned down the lights and began to play a war history video. Pamela looked over at Brian and was trying not to look too obvious. She was trying to get another look at those hazel eyes!

Lisa and Pamela's eyes met, and Lisa shook her head and giggled softly. Lisa's eyes were saying, *here we go AGAIN!*

This time, Pamela did not try to talk to the guy. She refused to get embarrassed for a second time. But of course, she had to figure out how to get his attention! Pamela continued sneaking glances at Brian. She could not get over those eyes! Brian's eyes were so captivating, and his brown tanned skin made them pop even more. *Focus girl, focus,* Pamela thought to herself. She already did not really care for History class but being distracted made it even more unbearable.

Pamela felt a light tap on her shoulder. She turned around and Lisa passed her a note. The note read: *I know you think Brian is cute. Are you going to try to talk to him today?* Pamela wrote her response and discretely passed the note back to Lisa. Lisa opened it and read Pamela's response and giggled.

The movie ended and the entire class was almost asleep. "So, what did you all think of the film?" Mr. Williams asked the students. Hidden within all the mumbles, one person yelled, "It was interesting!" Everyone let out a huge sigh because they all knew who had said it. There was always one suck-up in the class. Everyone rushed to pack up their belongings, so they could be ready to rush out the door once the bell rang.

RING! RING! RING!

While most of the kids flew out of the classroom, Lisa and Mya hurried to catch up to Pamela and pulled her hoodie over her head. "Not cool, guys!" Pamela said with a smile, trying not to look embarrassed or upset. Hundreds of tiny pieces of rolled up notebook paper had fallen all over her and got stuck in her curly hair. The two girls ran out of the classroom, leaving Pamela to clean up the mess. Pamela tidied it up in a hurry, so Brian would not see her. Too late! Brian walked past her, and now she was upset. *Why would they embarrass me in front of him like that? Were they trying to stop me from making a fool of myself by trying to talk to him?*

During the next week, Pamela tried to keep a low profile at school. She wanted all thoughts of that little paper ball prank to become old news. Pamela, Lisa, and Mya met up at the atrium for lunch and began discussing their plans for the prom.

"I already have my dress picked out!" exclaimed Mya.

"I don't have one yet," replied Lisa.

"Me neither," Pamela said.

Mya began bragging about her dress and describing every detail of it to the group. "It is floor length, red, and has crystals on it. The material is satin, and it has four thin crisscross straps in the back, and it has a slit."

"Oooh, that sounds so pretty!" Pamela said. Pamela did not like to bring attention to herself, so she thought about wearing a simple black dress to the

49

prom. "Do y'all have dates yet?" Pamela asked.

"Girl, you know I do," Mya proudly said.

"I'm going with Abe from Math class," Lisa said.

Pamela looked down and sighed. "We know who you WANT to go with!" Lisa giggled.

"He's so quiet and never tries to talk to me. Maybe he's waiting for me to hint that I like him or maybe he wants me to ask him?" Pamela told the girls. The girls rolled their eyes and told Pamela to let it go.

That night, Pamela took out some crafting supplies. She had fabric, yarn, beads, and a thick needle. Sarah walked into the room and saw Pamela on the floor with all the items. "What are you making, hun?" Sarah asked her.

"I'm making pants from scratch!" Pamela said excitedly.

"Do you need any help?" Sarah offered.

"No, thank you. I am okay, Ma," Pamela said. Sarah left her to it and Pamela began to get to work. First, she placed a pair of jeans on the floor to use as a pattern. She placed the thick, light brown jean fabric under the jeans, traced a rough outline on the fabric and then threw the jeans onto her bed. Next, she cut out the pattern and hand-sewed the two large pieces together. She sewed up all four sides but left the waist area untouched. She tried them on and was so proud of herself! She could wear these to school!

Now, it was time to add the beads. She took the white pencil and began to freehand her artwork on the left pant leg, adding lettering on the right pant leg. She grabbed black yarn and began to hand stitch the outline of her design and each of the letters. After that, she organized her beads and started to hand-sew each glass bead, one at a time, onto the fabric. The beads were a light brown caramel color and were about the size of sunflower seeds. It took Pamela hours to sew all of the beads. She was so excited to complete these pants the same night, that she almost missed dinner. She ate quickly and went back to her room. Hours went by and she kept on sewing. By then, it was almost midnight and she was so sleepy. She had a small spot left to add beads to, so she pushed herself to get it done.

The next morning, Pamela was so exhausted, but the excitement of wearing her pants to school gave her all the energy in the world!

"Good morning, hun," Sarah said sweetly to Pamela.

"Good morning, Ma," Pamela responded with a huge smile.

"How did your pants turn out and how late did you stay up last night?" Sarah asked.

"I finished them, and they are so cool! I think I was up until a little past midnight," Pamela admitted. Sarah was not thrilled about Pamela not getting proper rest but knew her daughter wouldn't have been able to sleep anyway if she had not completed her project.

Sarah looked at the pants and saw the design. "Honey, are you sure you want to wear these to school? Maybe you should just keep them here. You may not get the response that you want, and the pants may not last long, because you did not finish sewing them properly."

"It's okay. I really want to wear them. I'll wear leggings under them just in case," Pamela responded.

"I'm sorry, honey, I know you spent all of that time working on them, but you can't wear them to school. Go change your clothes. It's for the best...trust me," Sarah said.

Pamela frowned and went back into her room to change her clothes. She was disappointed and a little sad. *I have to wear them! Even if they only last for today. I don't care,* Pamela thought. She took the pants and tossed them onto her bed. She found another pair of jeans and put them on. While putting her shoes back on, she looked back at her beaded pants. She was deciding whether to leave them there or take them to school. She had butterflies in her stomach and a gut feeling but she ignored it. She grabbed her pants and hid them deep down in the bottom her backpack. *I'll change into these once I get to school*, she thought. She left her room and headed to the front door. Sarah looked Pamela over and told her she looked beautiful and that she was sorry that she could not allow her to wear those pants to school.

"It's okay," Pamela said.

Pamela arrived at school and kissed her mom goodbye. She ran to the bathroom so she could quickly change into her pants before the first bell rang. She changed into her new outfit and placed her original outfit into her backpack. Pamela proudly walked out of the bathroom and met up with the group in the hallway.

"Did you make those pants?" Mya asked.

"You know she did. She's always making stuff," Lisa replied. Lisa and Mya looked at the design and read the words on her pants. "Are you sure you want to wear those all day, Pamela?" asked Lisa.

"Yeah! It took me forever to make them and I WILL wear them!" Pamela said proudly.

The group started laughing and Lisa said, "Okay, but wearing them won't make him like you." She laughed.

"Whatever. Just watch. Once he sees that I made these for him, he will definitely want to take me to the prom!" Pamela said.

All morning, Pamela received nice compliments on her pants. She was grateful for the compliments, but these pants had one purpose and one purpose only. The girls met up in history class and waited outside for the bell to ring.

"Pamela, are you SURE you want to wear those pants in class? You still have time to change really quick!" Lisa encouraged.

"Nope! I want him to see them!" Pamela said.

As the other kids started walking in, they looked at Pamela's pants and started giggling. Everyone knew who she had made those pants for! Pamela just kept a straight face. She was trying to act like her pants were no big deal and did not want the kids to see how excited she was to show off her pants.

"There he is. He's coming," Lisa said while chuckling. Brian walked up to the door, glanced down at Pamela's pants, and did not say a word! But his facial expression said it all.

RED FLAG!

Pamela looked at Lisa, confused, and Lisa shrugged her shoulders. They both walked into the classroom and all eyes were on Pamela. Okay, now she was starting to get less excited and feel more embarrassed by the minute. During the entire class, she could not focus. Why didn't he like her pants? He had to know that she made those pants for him. Why wasn't he impressed? She looked down at her pants and tried to figure out what he did not like. She first looked at the design of the eye. It had the black outline, black eye lashes, black pupil and the light brown beads sparkled perfectly. It looked exactly like his eye. Then, she stretched out her leg to look at the lettering. All the letters were black, equally sized and spaced, and they spelled out, P-R-E-T-T-Y E-Y-E-S. She did not misspell anything. *There is nothing wrong with the pants! They look great! If I were him, I would be super impressed,* Pamela thought.

It was now almost time for class to end. Pamela was wondering if Brian would talk to her after class. Maybe he was just surprised and did not know what to say? Maybe he was just being shy?

RING! RING! RING!

Everyone rushed to the door and Pamela took her time leaving. Brian stood up, grabbed his stuff, and walked right by Pamela while giving her a strange look! *Wow...* Pamela thought to herself. *I worked so hard to make these pants for him and not one word!? I cannot believe I wasted my time. I should have listened to my mom and left the pants at home! Ugh!*

Lisa got up and said, "Are you okay?"

Pamela looked a little sad and said, "Yeah, I'm okay. I wish I didn't wear these stupid pants." Lisa looked down at the pants and saw some yard hanging. Pamela looked down to see what Lisa was looking at and saw the yarn strand, too. Pamela pulled on the strand and *ZIP. ZIP. ZIP.* The stitches came apart! The pants started slipping off Pamela's body and she quickly stepped out of them and pulled on her original pants from that morning.

"It's a good thing you had those leggings on underneath!" Lisa said.

They both walked out of the classroom and Pamela tried to hide her embarrassment through the rest of the day.

RING! RING! RING!

The final bell rang and Pamela could not wait to get home, so she could finally cry. She had been holding it in all day! Pamela walked to the pickup area and Sarah pulled up and honked.

"Hey, hun. How was school today?" Sarah asked.

"It was okay, just a regular day," Pamela said. Pamela was quiet the whole ride home, replaying the day repeatedly.

"Are you okay?" Sarah asked.

"Yeah, I'm just tired," Pamela responded. They arrived home and Pamela rushed to her room. She quickly pulled out her destroyed pants and threw them in the closet. She did not want her mom to find out that she wore them to school when she'd told her not to.

While sitting on the bed she thought, *I am not even in the friend-zone with Brian. He doesn't want to have anything to do with me. What is going on with these guys? First Axel and now Brian.* She worked on her homework and then watched some music videos before dinner, to get her mind off things and get into a better mood. *Okay, I am so done with these high school guys. They don't know how to appreciate a girl like me!*

Pamela decided to focus on the fun summer ahead and prepare for the summer program that she'd signed up for. The program allowed students from different high schools to have the on-campus university experience. For about three months, the students took college-level classes and of course, Pamela met a guy. But this time,

she focused on herself and decided not to even bother
with him.

6 THE POKER FACE AND THE JOCK WITH POTENTIAL

The rest of the summer flew by and Pamela had clearly moved on from Brian. Every time he walked past her; she did not even bat an eye. She couldn't have cared less if he came to class or not. Before class started, Pamela's friend, Tony, came to talk to her. She was excited to see him because she did not have any classes with him this year.

"Hey Pamela, how are you?" he asked.

"I'm doing okay. It's good to see you. It's been a while!"

He smiled big and said, "I've missed you, girl!"

Pamela smiled and tried to act cool. She had always had a crush on him but did not want to ruin the friendship that they had. They had been friends for years and had fun times. Their favorite memories were of the times in the show choir at Bishop Ward Middle School.

"Hey, do you remember when Mrs. Ivy used to give us snacks at the end of each rehearsal?" Pamela said while giggling.

"Heck yeah! We all used to run to the table to get the cake rolls. Those were everyone's favorite!" Tony said.

RING! RING! RING!

The first period bell rang. "I have to go. Hope to see you again soon. My football practices have been rescheduled, so I will be able to see you more often before class," Tony said.

"Okay! That sounds great," Pamela said. She walked into class and was greeted by a stare and a smirk from Lisa and Mya.

"What!?" Pamela said. The two girls just shook their heads and giggled. "We're just friends y'all. You know that," Pamela said.

Of course, they knew they were friends, but they also knew that Pamela had secretly liked him all these years.

"I wonder why he is coming around now?" Pamela asked the girls.

Lisa replied, "Maybe he misses you? Maybe he likes you now?"

Pamela smiled and said, "You really think so?!"

Lisa shook her head. "Why do you care? I thought y'all were just friends?"

"Okay, okay, fine. I do wish he liked me. It would be nice to have someone like me back for a change," Pamela said.

Lisa gently placed her hand on Pamela's shoulder and said, "Don't worry friend. One day the right guy will come along. You are such a great girl and you deserve the best guy in the world!"

Mr. Williams walked in and told the class to get ready to take a lot of notes that day, because he had a lot of information to cover. The class let out a huge sigh. They knew that there was no time to joke and play during class today. When Mr. Williams gave notes, he ran through the projector slides like a mad man! If you pause for even a second to erase a word, sneeze, or blink, you have lost a whole slide of notes! Pamela was in trouble now. She kept catching herself daydreaming about Tony and every time she caught herself, she realized how far behind she was with the notes! *Hopefully, someone will just let me copy their notes later,* she thought. She continued thinking about Tony. *Does he like me? If I write him a letter, will he write me back? I must test the waters and see if he likes me likes me or if he is just being friendly as usual.*

RING! RING! RING!

Pamela looked down at her notes and saw she

only had like two pages worth, while everyone else had four to five! Pamela was not worried, she finally came up with her game plan for figuring out Tony's feelings for her, so she was okay.

Pamela got through her other classes and then it was lunch time. She met up with Lisa and Mya at their usual spot and waited for her friend, Ted, to grab their order of cheese fries. Ted was such a gentleman and did not mind grabbing their lunch. He always did things for the girls, such as carrying books —or was he just a nice guy? Lisa and Mya were probably shocked that Pamela did not like him in that way! Or maybe they were not shocked. Pamela did seem to gravitate toward mysterious, bad boy types.

"What are you doing sitting on the ground?" Mya asked Pamela.

"I'm writing a letter," Pamela replied.

Lisa shook her head and giggled. "Let me guess. You're writing Tony a letter?"

Pamela looked up with a smirk and said, "Yes, so what? I can write a friend a letter, can't I?"

The girls saw right through her. "We know you have always liked him. Just tell him in the letter. We can give it to him for you!" Mya said.

"Fine. I will tell him, and I will give him the letter myself. I don't want you to read it!" Pamela said jokingly.

It took Pamela the entire lunch period to write the note. She wanted to make sure it was perfect. It read:

Hey Tony, what's up? I am glad I was able to see you today. You have been so busy with football practice. How is football going? Also, I was just wondering, what kind of snacks do you like? I could bring you some the next time I see you, if you want.

-Pamela

She carefully re-read the note, to make sure she didn't reveal too much of her soul in one letter. She neatly folded the note into a triangle shape and tucked the loose corner into the side. She quickly slipped the note into her backpack, while the girls tried to snatch it from her. She knew they would try to do that. Pamela had minutes to eat. She scarfed down her cold cheese fries and walked over to the trash can to toss out the empty paper tray.

As she walked back toward the girls, Pamela felt a sensation as if one of the small rubber bands in her hair was tearing and pulling at her hair strands.

"Ouch!" she said, while trying to pull out the rubber band. She brought her hand down to inspect the damaged rubber band and was in shock! She looked at her clasped fingers and saw yellow and black. That was not her rubber band at all—it was a wasp! "OMG! OMG! Ouch!" Pamela screamed as she dropped the wasp in a panic.

"What's wrong?" Lisa asked.

Pamela walked over to them, crying, and said, "A wasp just stung me on the top of my head!"

Lisa gently put her hand on Pamela's shoulder and said, "You'll be okay, friend. I'll take you to the nurse."

Mya told Pamela, "I hope you feel better!" and all Pamela could do was wave bye. Lisa grabbed her stuff and Pamela grabbed her backpack and they both headed to the nurse.

"How can I help you ladies?" Nurse Betty asked.

"Pamela just got stung by one of those wasps in the atrium," Lisa explained.

"Yes, we have a bad wasp problem this year and have had a few stings in the past week," Nurse Betty said.

RING! RING! RING!

The lunch bell rang, and it was time for everyone to start heading to their next class. Lisa hugged Pamela and said, "I have to go, but I will meet up with you after class to check on you. Do you want me to give him your note? I usually see him in the halls around this time."

Pamela, still in tears, just nodded her head up and down to say okay. Lisa searched through Pamela's backpack and found the note and walked out. Nurse Betty prepared some ice chips in a clear baggie and wrapped it in a thin, brown paper towel. "Okay, dear.

Place this icepack on your head on and off for a few minutes at a time. Are you okay to go to your next class?"

"Uh huh. I have art class next," Pamela murmured. Art was one of her favorite classes, because not only did she love art, but her teacher, Ms. Lisette, was so nice and understanding. She knew she would allow her to just relax and do what she could in class today. Pamela thanked the nurse and went to class.

Pamela walked slowly to her art class. Her head was pounding and throbbing with every step. She tried to open the door, but it took too much energy. She knocked on the door and Ms. Lisette opened it for her.

"What's wrong, Pamela? What happened?" Ms. Lisette asked.

Pamela looked up with tears running down her cheeks and said, "I just got stung on the top of my head by one of those wasps in the atrium."

Ms. Lisette gave her a hug and guided her to her seat. "We have a drawing assignment today, but you can take a rest for ten minutes and then see if you can try to work on it some."

Pamela reached for her colored pencil, to see if she could at least try to draw something. Two minutes went by and she suddenly dropped the pencil on the table. "Ooowww," Pamela moaned.

The guy next to her turned and said, "Wow, it hurts that bad huh?"

Pamela could not even turn her head. "Yes, my head is throbbing so bad!" Pamela slowly breathed in and out. She reached for her pencil again, to show Ms. Lisette that she was trying. She did not want her to think she was taking advantage of her kindness.

Pamela bravely pushed through the rest of the class. There were moments left in the period and she was able to get half of her drawing done.

RING! RING! RING! It was time to go to her next class.

"You did an excellent job today, Pamela, and I hope you feel better soon." Ms. Lisette said.

"Thank you," Pamela said softly. She grabbed her backpack and slowly left the classroom. She continued through the hallway and was greeted by Lisa.

"Are you okay? I went by the nurse's office and didn't see you there. Nurse Betty told me that you went to class. Maybe you should ask if you can go home early?"

Pamela looked up and said, "I'm okay, but my head is still pounding some. It is okay, though. I can make it."

Lisa handed her a note. "What's this?" Pamela asked.

"I just saw Tony again. He asked me how you were doing, and he told me to give this to you!" Lisa said with excitement. Pamela tried to smile, but it hurt to do so. She could not believe he wrote her back so fast. Did this prove that he liked her? She took the note from Lisa and tried to read it before walking the rest of the way to her next class. The note read:

Hey Pamela. Lisa told me that you were stung by one of the wasps. I am so sorry. I hope you feel better soon! I am glad that I was able to see you, too. Practice has been going great and we hope to win next week's game. My favorite thing to eat is bacon, but you do not have to bring me any! I was wondering, are you going to prom? I would love to take you!

– Tony

Pamela's excitement was through the roof and the adrenalin seemed to ease her pain from the wasp sting! Lisa saw Pamela's eyes light up and asked, "What does it say? It must be good!"

Pamela whispered in her ear, "He asked me to prom!"

Lisa hugged her and said, "Congrats, friend. I am so happy for you! I guess he does like you!" Lisa looked at her watch and noticed they only had moments to get to class. "Girl, we're going to be late! Hurry!" So, they both raced to class, barely making it on time. Of course, Pamela could not concentrate through any of her classes for the rest of the day.

It was finally time for school to let out. The final bell rang, and everyone rushed out the doors. Pamela met up with the group briefly to say goodbye and walked over to the pickup area to wait for her mom. Her mom pulled up and noticed that Pamela had been crying. "What happened, Hun!? It looks like you've been crying!"

"I'm okay now; I was stung by a wasp earlier today," Pamela said. After a few minutes of reassuring her mom that she was okay, they headed home. "Guess what, Ma?" Pamela said.

"What's up?" Sarah asked.

"Do you remember Tony from show choir back in middle school? He asked me to prom!" Pamela exclaimed.

"That's great! I'm so happy for you. I know that you've liked him for a long time!" Sarah said.

"I'm so happy! The prom is in a couple of weeks, so I still have time to pick the perfect dress!" Pamela said.

They arrived at home and Pamela read his note again. She got butterflies in her stomach every time she pictured herself dancing with Tony at the prom. *I wonder what colors we should wear? Will he pick me up? Will he kiss me?* she wondered. Pamela was exhausted from the day and sleepiness was starting to creep in. "Owww," she murmured.

Now, a nagging pain was coming back. She went to the dining room and sat down. "Dinner is almost ready. You can take some medicine after you eat and go straight to bed," Sarah said.

While waiting, Pamela was thinking of what to write Tony in her next letter. She had to give him an answer and had to ask him if they were a couple or just friends. She did not want to get her hopes up, if he was just being nice. "Here you go, Hun." Sarah placed a plate in front of Pamela. Pamela ate most of her food, took some medicine and went to her room. She wrote the note to Tony and then went to sleep.

The next morning, Pamela re-read her note to make sure it sounded okay. She put it in her backpack and headed into the dining room for breakfast. Perfect! Sarah had made eggs, grits, and bacon. They both sat down to eat, and Pamela sneaked two strips of bacon into a paper towel and placed it in her backpack.

"Okay, let's go," Sarah said. They both placed their dishes in the sink and walked out the door. On the way to school, Sarah sniffed a couple times. "Do you smell bacon?"

Pamela shook her head no and smiled. She was hoping her mom did not find out she had bacon in her backpack! That would be so embarrassing. They arrived at the school and said goodbye. Sarah drove off and Pamela started walking to the building.

She entered the hallway and saw Tony. He walked up to her and gave her a hug! Pamela hugged him back and breathed him in!

"How are you this morning?" he asked.

"I'm okay. The sting doesn't hurt anymore,"

Pamela said. She reached into her backpack and pulled out the letter and the bacon wrapped in the paper towel. "Here, I wrote you back and brought you these."

He took the letter and took the paper towel. He unwrapped it, smiled at Pamela and laughed. "Thank you," he said, while eating the bacon.

RING! RING! RING!

It was time for first period to start, so everyone rushed to class, and Tony waved goodbye to Pamela. It was a little warm that day, so Pamela put her jacket into the locker that she sometimes shared with her friend Angelica. Her locker was closer to Pamela's next class than Pamela's own locker was.

Class passed quickly and it was almost time to leave. "What did you give him?" Mya asked as she started packing up her stuff.

"A note and some bacon. He told me he likes bacon," Pamela said.

Lisa giggled and asked, "You actually gave him bacon!?"

All three of them laughed. "So, are y'all together now?" Lisa asked Pamela.

"I guess so. I told him yes to prom and he gave me a hug and ate the bacon, so I think we are!" she said. The bell rang and everyone rushed out the door. As Pamela walked out, she saw some people looking at her and there was a lot of chatter. Word got around fast, especially when it came to one of the popular guys at the school. Pamela walked to Angelica's locker and acted like the stares didn't bother her. She was sure people were wondering why he would want the quiet girl to be his girlfriend. His ex-girlfriend, Shay, was nothing like Pamela, and people already wondered why they broke up. Pamela opened the locker and looked for her jacket.

Where is my jacket? I thought I put it in here, she thought. She found her friend Angelica and asked her if she had seen her jacket. "No, I haven't seen it, but Shay shares that locker with me sometimes, too. I will ask her if she saw it."

Pamela thanked her and thought, *you have got to be kidding me. Why didn't she tell me that another person knew the combination to her locker?*

The next class flew by and afterwards, Pamela went back to check the locker again. She paused and saw something out of the corer of her eye. Something was in the water fountain. She looked over and saw a large pile of white fabric covered in dark grey dirt, sitting in the water fountain. She carefully picked it up to examine it. She looked at the tag and confirmed that it was her jacket! The worst part was that it was not HER jacket, but rather her mom's jacket that she had borrowed! Pamela's stomach dropped and she became angry while laughing at the same time. *There is no way Shay did this. That is so childish!* She was mad that the jacket was ruined, but at the same time, it made her feel good, because this meant it was official— word was going around that Tony and Pamela were boyfriend and girlfriend! Pamela did not make a big fuss over the jacket and did not confront Shay about it either. Over the next several weeks, she just walked the halls with Tony every chance she could, to show everyone that she was happy and unbothered.

"Prom Night! It's finally happening!" Mya joyfully exclaimed. Everyone was so excited and could hardly focus on their classes. Everywhere you turned, you could see girls gushing over what their dresses looked like, their dates, and their after-prom plans.

"Is Tony picking you up tonight?" Lisa asked Pamela.

"No, he said he wants to meet me there, so my mom will drop me off and pick me up," Pamela said.

RED FLAG! Lisa and Mya looked confused. "Why would he not pick you up?" Lisa asked. Pamela shrugged. All day, Pamela was trying to figure out why he just wanted to meet her at prom. This was not the fairytale she had in mind. *Maybe he has something special planned for when he sees me? Maybe he needed the extra time to get his surprise ready?* Pamela thought.

SNAP! SNAP! SNAP!

"Mooooooommmmmm," Pamela groaned, as her mom took a million photos.

"Come on, hun. Just one more. Stand over there by the flowers!" *SNAP! SNAP!* Pamela was ready but nervous. She and her mom hopped in the car and drove to the hotel, where the prom was being held. "Have fun! I love you!" Sarah told Pamela.

"Thank you! I love you, too!" Pamela said. As Sarah drove off, Pamela started walking towards the doors. She could hear the loud, muffled music and feel the thump of the bass. No sign of Tony and Pamela had lied to her mom when she told her that Tony texted her that he was there and waiting.

She walked in and looked around. She saw Mya at the photo booth with her date and saw Lisa at one of the tables with her date. Pamela walked around the ballroom, pretending to say hi to some friends throughout the crowd; all the while, she was really searching for Tony. After a few minutes, she gave up and went to sit with Lisa.

Fifteen minutes passed and Tony strolled through the door, empty handed.

"Hey, sorry I'm late," he said to Pamela, with no further explanation.

RED FLAG. Pamela put on a blank face and told him it was okay. They danced a few times, but not to any slow songs. Every time a slow song came on, he suddenly had to sit down or go to the restroom. *What is going on with him? He is not being romantic at all. Doesn't pick me up, no corsage, no flowers, no hug...nothing!* Pamela was confused.

"Last song of the night!" the *DJ* announced.

72

Okay, he has to dance to this slow song. This is the last song! Pamela thought. Tony grabbed her hand and they walked to the dance floor. As they danced, Pamela continued to fill with sadness. There was a huge space between them, and he barely looked at her.

"I have to tell you something," Tony confessed. Pamela started feeling anxious; she knew this was not good news and was probably why he had been acting so distant that night.

"Okay, what is it?" she asked.

He looked at her and said, "I like you, but I just want to stay friends. We are going to be in college in a few months and I want to keep my options open. I'm sorry," Tony confessed.

Pamela's eyes teared up and she quietly said, "Wow. Why couldn't you tell me this before? All this time, I thought we were boyfriend and girlfriend."

Pamela could not finish the dance and they both went to sit down. Mya and Lisa looked over to Pamela from the dance floor and knew something was wrong. The music cut off and the bright white lights turned on. "Have a good night and be safe everyone!" The *DJ* announced. Everyone left the ballroom and the girls hung around outside with Pamela to wait for her mom.

"What happened, friend?" Lisa asked Pamela.

Pamela did not want to start crying again. "Tony does not want to be with me. I'll call you guys tomorrow."

The girls stood there, in shock. Pamela and her mom drove off and then Pamela started crying her eyes out to her mom. She explained what happened and her mom tried to make her feel better. "I know it hurts a lot now, but I promise it will get better with a little time, plus with college just around the corner, you will be able to have a fresh start."

7 THE SMIRK AND THE WILD FLIRT

"Thank you, handsome," Pamela said cutely to the student government president as he handed her a flyer.

He smiled ear to ear, and said, "Thank you beautiful." He was asking her to vote for him for president and Pamela was trying to put herself out there. 'No fear' was her new motto. Now that she was a college woman, she felt it was time for her to try to overcome her shyness.

Lisa looked over at Pamela and said, "I'm proud of you friend! Wait for it...wait for it. He is going to come and ask for your number, just watch!"

"Hey, can I have your number!?" the guy asked.

"Sure, handsome!" Pamela said back.

He ran over, put her number in his phone and said, "You ladies have a nice day!"

Lisa and Pamela giggled and headed to the game room. They both had a rough first class and decided to go exploring.

"Man, I wish Mya hadn't had to move away to go to college," Pamela said.

"Me, too. I miss her a lot," Lisa said.

They stopped and posed for a selfie together. Lisa took the picture with her cell phone and sent it to Mya with a message that read, *We miss ya girlie! ...and yes, Pamela talked to a cute guy already! LOL.*

They continued to walk along the longest sidewalk on campus. It stretched all the way from the Fine Arts building to the game room across the field. Once they finally arrived at the game room, they saw a part time job opening to work both there and for the office next door.

"This could be fun!" Pamela said. She called the number on the flyer and set up a meeting for the next morning. They walked in and looked to the left, to the west side of the room. There was a TV on the wall with some bean bag chairs crowding the area. That was the gaming spot. To the right of that, there were a few pool tables. To the north side of the room, there was a ping pong table and to the south there was a large, built-in desk near the door. The woman at the desk, named Ms. Jones, kindly greeted them as they walked past her. Finally, to the east, there was a partial glass wall and beyond that was a large sitting area where most of the students were hanging out. There was a sofa, a couple small tables with chairs, and a huge flat screen TV on the wall.

"This place is so cool!" Pamela said. "I hope I get to work in here. This would be great to help me meet new people and get over my shyness!" Lisa agreed and they both watched a little TV before they had to get to their next class.

Pamela's phone alarm went off. No more school bells to help remind them when classes ended and began. They both got up and headed towards the door. Pamela looked over at the desk and noticed a guy now working behind it, wearing a black shirt with a Puerto Rican flag on it. "Wait, he wasn't there when we came in. He's so hot!" Pamela whispered to Lisa.

"Oh, now you REALLY want to work here, huh?" Lisa said jokingly.

The next morning after class, they made their way to the game room again. No sign of the student president and Pamela did not receive a call or a text from him. She figured he was too busy with campaigning and other responsibilities, so she was okay with that. Lisa walked into the game room, while Pamela went to the office next door for an interview.

"Good luck, friend!" Lisa said to Pamela. The interview took fifteen minutes and Pamela got the job! Ms. Katy, the interviewer, told Pamela about her responsibilities and part-time work hours. Every day, she would have to supervise the game room alongside Ms. Jones. Her other tasks included going around campus and removing old flyers from the cylindrical towers in all the buildings, creating student ID badges, and some data entry work. Pamela was so excited and liked that she would have different tasks, so it would never get boring. Ms. Katy walked back into the game room with Pamela and introduced her to Ms. Jones before returning to her office.

"It is nice to meet you, Pamela. Let me show you what you will be doing," Ms. Jones said.

Afterward, Pamela thanked Ms. Jones and went to sit with Lisa to tell her the good news. She had a few minutes, before she had to start her first shift. Lisa congratulated Pamela and gave her a big hug. Pamela got back up and walked back towards the desk. As Pamela approached the desk, the cute guy walked through the door and walked behind the desk, too.

"Hey, I'm Rio. I see we will be working together now, huh?" the cute guy said.

Pamela grinned and replied, "Yup, I'm just starting today." Rio brushed up against her arm, while reaching for a pen for the sign-in sheet. He smiled and Pamela smiled back. Ms. Jones gave them both the side-eye and grinned. She could clearly see that there was chemistry between these two!

For the next hour and a half of her shift, Pamela tried to get to know Rio better, while also trying to look professional. He was incredibly open and engaged in the conversation and asked her questions, too. Lisa kept glancing over at Pamela and smirking from where she sat over in the common area. She could see Pamela had been sucked into his web already! Pamela prepared to clock out and Rio grabbed her hand.

"Hey, do you want to go out tonight? We can go to the movies or something," he asked.

Pamela quickly answered, "Sure, I'd like that." She gave him her number. Then she waived bye to Lisa and headed to her last class of the day. This college scheduling was great. Every other day was a short day for her and today was one of them. She would have plenty of time to get ready for her date tonight.

BING! Pamela received a text from Rio that said, *I'm outside.*

"Okay, Ma, he's here. I'll see you later," Pamela said. Pamela still lived at home with her mom. She did not see the point in wasting money living on campus when she could stay home for free! Plus, Sarah did not mind keeping her baby girl around a little longer either. "Okay, hun. Have fun and be safe." Pamela grabbed her purse and walked out the door.

CHIRP! CHIRP! While remaining in the car, Rio unlocked the doors from the inside. Pamela walked up to the passenger car door and opened it.

RED FLAG. *Okay, I see he is not a gentleman...strike one,* Pamela thought. Pamela was still a little shy and was having a hard time finding things to talk about. Rio tried to break her out of her shell and it eventually worked. They arrived at the movies and walked up to the concession stand.

"Do you want some popcorn and a drink? Order anything you want," Rio said to her. They both put in their orders and Rio paid with his card. *Okay, okay. He is a gentleman. Usually, guys make me pay for half!* Pamela thought. Pamela's views on dating etiquette seemed to be old-fashioned to most, but she didn't want to lower her standards just to keep up with the times. They grabbed their food and headed into theater number 7. The whole time they were holding hands, and he leaned in and kissed her on the cheek a couple times. Pamela felt so good, she could hardly pay attention to the movie.

The movie ended and hand-in-hand, they left the theater. He drove her home and when they got there, he tried to make out with her in the car. Pamela was hesitant at first, because they were parked in front of her mom's house, but the excitement was too much! She was the good girl, and this was a big step for her! Thirty minutes went by and Pamela paused. "I have to go," she said sweetly.

"Can you stay just a few more minutes?" Rio asked.

"I can't. It's late," Pamela said. She was looking in the visor mirror to make sure she still looked presentable and then got out of the car. Rio waved and said goodnight, while Pamela walked into the house, then he drove away. Pamela walked quietly past her mom's room, trying not to wake her. Her mom had to go to work early in the morning.

"Hey hun, how did it go?" Sarah murmured while half asleep.

"It was fun," Pamela said. They both said goodnight and Pamela went to bed.

Lisa and Pamela met up the next morning to walk to the game room together. "So, how was it?" Lisa asked.

"It was nice. We had fun," Pamela said with a grin. As they kept walking, Pamela told Lisa all the hot details. Lisa was surprised that Pamela let loose a little for once. She was glad Pamela was having a little fun. They arrived at the game room and Lisa went to sit in her usual spot, while Pamela worked at the desk.

"Both of you have to clean the flyer stands today. Grab some trash bags and do as many as you can," Ms. Jones instructed. Rio and Pamela left and started at building C, which was right next door to the game room.

While ripping off the old flyers and posters, Rio asked Pamela some probing questions, "Do you drink? Do you go out to the club? Are you a virgin?" Pamela answered honestly and so did he. She liked that they were able to be open with each other so early in their relationship!

After two months of dating, the spark was still there. Rio was always finding new ways to test the limits with Pamela and get her to try fun things.

"Hey, come here," Rio pulled Pamela into an empty classroom while they were out pulling flyers. He laid her down on the teacher's desk and started kissing her. Pamela had never felt like this before! Her adrenalin was through the roof!

"What if someone passes by? What if a professor comes in!?" Pamela asked so many questions, it ruined the moment. Pamela was enjoying herself, but the good girl in her just would not allow her to go all in and have fun. "I'm sorry; I just can't," Pamela said.

Rio sighed and stood up. They both fixed their clothes and hair and continued to the next building. Rio was quiet the rest of the hour.

RED FLAG! Things were so awkward now. Pamela was bummed that she did not allow herself to have fun, but also felt relieved that they did not get caught. Having fun was not worth losing her job. They finished the last of the flyers in the building and walked back to the game room.

Ms. Jones gave them the side eye again. She knew there was tension between them. She had been working with Rio for a while and knew he was a little wild while Pamela was not.

Rio clocked out and Pamela stayed behind the desk, since she had a longer shift today. "Are you okay?" Ms. Jones asked.

"Yeah, I'm okay," Pamela answered. Ms. Jones smiled and left it at that. She did not want to pry. After an hour, Lisa went to class and gave Pamela the *I told you so* look after reading all of Pamela's texts, complaining about Rio. Pamela waved bye to her with a guilty look on her face. Lisa had warned her about this guy, but Pamela kept brushing her off.

As Lisa walked out, Ms. Jones' nephew, Ali, walked in. Ms. Jones introduced him to Pamela and told him that Pamela was feeling down. Ali struck up great conversation that cheered her right up. She had two hours left in her shift and they talked the entire time.

"Thanks for the chat, Ali. Have a good day, y'all," Pamela said to Ali and Mrs. Jones. She left the game room and went to the metal benches out front to wait for the bus to go home.

"Hello?" Pamela answered her phone.

"Hey what's up? It's Rio." Pamela stayed quiet. "Sorry about earlier, but I don't think we're going to work out," Rio continued.

"Why? Is it because I am too much of a good girl for you? Am I not fun enough for you?" Pamela responded sharply.

"I don't understand why you can't just have fun?" Rio said.

"Excuse me for trying to be responsible and for not wanting to get into trouble."

As Rio and Pamela continued to argue, Ali left the building and walked towards Pamela. He noticed that she looked unhappy and caught her eye and whispered, "Are you okay?"

Pamela shook her head no and gestured for him to sit down. After another minute or two, Pamela cut Rio off and said, "Look, I am sorry you feel that way, but I'm not going to change. I think it's best we just be friends." Then, she hung up.

Ali overheard enough to understand what was going on. "You deserve better than that. You need a guy who won't try to change you," Ali said kindly.

"You're right. Thank you," Pamela said. The bus pulled up and Pamela stood up. Ali offered her a hug and she hugged him gently. Then, Pamela got on the bus and watched him walk to his car. *He seems like a good guy, but he may be too nice for me*, Pamela thought.

8 THE SMIRK AND THE GENTLE CRUSH

"This is so awkward." Pamela said to Ali while they watched TV in the game room. It was almost time for her shift and Rio was at the desk, trying not to stare at them. As Pamela and Rio grew apart week-by-week, she and Ali had grown closer as friends. Rio and Pamela were polite to each other, but they were hardly friends.

"What's your favorite movie or cartoon?" Ali asked her, to change the subject.

"There was this movie I used to watch all the time when I was younger and it was about this guy who likes this woman, but the woman babysits these really bad kids," Pamela said.

"Oh, I know that movie! I know every word by heart. I used to watch it all the time, too!" Ali said.

They both started singing some of the theme

song and quoting several of the lines, just having a good old time. They did not care who was watching or laughing at them, they were in their own little world for a minute.

"Hi, beautiful," said a man with a deep voice.

Pamela got the chills and smiled. Who was that talking with that sultry, deep voice? She turned toward the door and saw this tall guy standing there with a chemistry textbook in his hand.

He walked over and introduced himself, gently grabbing Pamela's hand as he said, "I just wanted to take a moment to say hello to you and introduce myself. My name is Joe."

"Hi, Joe. It's nice to meet you and you have a lovely voice by the way," Pamela tried to say calmly. She did not want Ali to see that she was impressed by Joe. Ali was watching TV and Pamela was hoping that he did not notice what was going on. Ali was just a friend, and she did not want to hurt his feelings, but wanted to keep her options open, just in case.

"Thank you. I just wanted to introduce myself to you. I have to go study for a test that I have in an hour. You have a nice day now," Joe said. He waved goodbye to Ms. Jones and went to one of the tables to study. Ms. Jones gave Pamela the side-eye with a smirk.

Pamela looked at her and said, "He's clearly an older guy and I am not going to fall for that stunt he just pulled. He knew I was going to like being called beautiful with his alluring deep voice." Pamela LOVED his voice and was trying not to like him. He glanced over at her maybe one time and she glanced over at him quite a few more. She was trying to analyze him.

"Hey Pamela, I have to go to class and won't be able to see you for the rest of the day. Do you want to hang out later?" Ali asked her.

"I'd love to," Pamela said. Ali smiled and said goodbye to Pamela and Ms. Jones and left the game room.

An hour passed and Joe got up and gathered his stuff. He walked past the desk and told Pamela and Ms. Jones to have a nice day then left. *Hmm...he didn't try to exchange numbers or ask me out? It is kind of nice that he is not acting like most guys would,* Pamela thought to herself.

BING! Pamela received a text from Ali. It read: *Hey, let's meet at the bus stop outside of building C and I will take you to a secret spot where we can hang out. Meet me around 4.*

Pamela replied with a text that read: *Okay, sounds good. See you then.*

This would be the first time that they hung out alone. It would be a good chance to get to know each other and see if this could go anywhere.

"Do you all have a student ID?" Ms. Jones asked a group of people who just walked through the door. They did not look familiar.

87

"No, we're here to meet up with a friend," a guy in the group said.

"I'm sorry, but only students are allowed in here. If you are not a student, but you are visiting one, then the student needs to be with you," Ms. Jones explained.

"No problem. We will come back when he is out of class," the guy said. The group walked out.

"There's got to be an easier way to keep track of people," Pamela said to Ms. Jones. As of now, everyone who walked in had to sign-in on the sheet on the clipboard. Calling people over to the desk to ask them if they had an ID and having them sign-in had become a daunting task for Pamela. She could not believe Ms. Jones had been doing this for years.

"Don't worry, we don't have to do this for long. As a matter of fact, we are getting a card swipe and cameras installed tomorrow morning. The only time people will need to sign the sheet will be to check out the video game console," Ms. Jones explained. Pamela was relieved.

"Hey, Pam. Hey, Ms. Jones," Rio said with a smile as he walked in. He walked around to the other side of the desk and clocked in. Pamela and Ms. Jones looked at each other. They were wondering why he was such in a good mood.

"Did something happen today? You seem happy," Pamela asked.

"My dad is back home from his business trip and we are going on a fishing trip later today. We haven't been able to hang out in a long time."

Pamela gently put her hand on his shoulder and said, "Aw, that's so great to hear! I hope you two have fun."

Ms. Jones smiled and said that was nice. Pamela's shift was over, and it was time for her next class. "You both have a good day," she said. Pamela walked over to Building H to her art history class.

This class went by slowly. Pamela tried to find interesting things about the class, but it just wasn't for her. She wanted it to be over, so she could finally hang with Ali. *I wonder where the secret hangout spot is?* she thought. Pamela started daydreaming and that helped the time pass.

"Projects are due tomorrow. Have a good day," the professor announced. Class was over. Finally. Pamela walked across campus to meet up with Ali. She walked up to the bus stop and saw Ali sitting on the dark metal bench.

"How was class?" he asked her.

"It was okay, but glad it's done," Pamela said with a sigh.

"Are you ready to see the spot?" he asked her. Pamela nodded her head yes and they walked to his car. He opened the passenger car door for her. She got in the car and smiled as he walked around the car to get in the driver's seat; she was happy that he was a gentleman. He pulled out of the parking spot and slowly grabbed Pamela's hand to hold in his. Their fingers intertwined and Pamela started to get butterflies in her stomach. She was caught off guard, in a good way, by her reaction. She was starting to feel *that* way about him. Interesting.

The spot was only a few minutes away from campus. Pamela stared out of the window and watched the skinny trees go by, looking like blurs. Suddenly, the car slowed, and Ali drove up to what looked like an unfinished road and underpass. Pamela was hesitant to get out of the car but was curious to see what he had planned. They both got out and Ali led her to the light grey concrete picnic table.

"This is a cool spot. How did you find it?" Pamela asked.

"I was driving around one day and saw some kids hanging out here," he said. He gently grabbed her hand. Pamela sat on the table and Ali sat on the seat of the bench. "So, what do you think of me?" Ali asked Pamela.

"I think you are a nice guy, and we have fun together," Pamela responded sweetly. Ali slowly moved in closer to Pamela and leaned in to kiss her. The kiss was soft and passionate and sweet all at the same time. Pamela was pleasantly surprised and was not expecting that! "Wow," Pamela said.

"What's wrong? Was that too fast, too soon?"

Ali asked her.

"Nothing is wrong. You're just an amazing kisser! To be honest, I was not expecting that," Pamela admitted.

Ali laughed and said, "I'm glad you think so and you are a great kisser as well."

Pamela had a flashback to Chase and giggled because he seemed to have taught her well!

"What's so funny?" Ali asked her with a smile.

"Oh, nothing. I'm still surprised over what just happened," she said. Pamela looked at her phone and saw what time it was. "I have to get home. I have a project for my art history class that is due tomorrow and I have to finish it up." They both got up and walked to the car. He opened the door for her and leaned in to kiss her again. They kissed for another minute or two and then Pamela jokingly pushed him off and told him they really needed to go. He drove her back to the game room and waited with her. Her next class was in about twenty minutes. He watched TV, while Pamela talked with Ms. Jones.

"Hey stranger! I haven't seen you here in a while, girl!" Pamela said. Lisa had just walked in after not hanging out in the game room in weeks.

"Hey, friend. Classes have been crazy, and I just haven't had time to drop by," Lisa said.

"I'm sorry, girl. I have to go to class soon, but I

can come chat if you're still here when I get back," Pamela told her.

Lisa said, "That sounds good," and walked over to her spot on the sofa to watch TV.

Ms. Jones jokingly tapped Pamela on the shoulder. Pamela looked over at her and Ali came to the desk. Ms. Jones obviously knew something had happened between the two of them.

"Hey what's up, y'all?" Ali said to them. Ms. Jones and Pamela waved and smiled. "When your class is over, do you want to hang out?" Ali asked Pamela.

"Yeah, but first, I have to talk to my best friend. I haven't seen her in a while," she said.

"No problem! I'll just hang around a bit while you two catch up." Ali said. He walked over to one of the small tables near the TV. Pamela went to class.

Pamela returned to the game room and walked over to Lisa, who was sitting there with her arms crossed. She was cold and left her jacket at home. "Are you okay?" Pamela asked her.

Lisa was incredibly quiet and assured her she was okay. Lisa was acting strange.

"Hey pretty lady," a male voice said. Lisa and Pamela turned around to see whom it was. Lisa smirked and Pamela was in disbelief. It was Jerome! Pamela had had a brief crush on him after they met in one of her classes, but he didn't seem to feel the same way. He clearly was not talking to Pamela now either, so who was he talking to? "Are you going to come hang with me or what?" Jerome said while looking at Lisa.

Pamela looked over at Ali and she must have had a sad look on her face, because Ali just shook his head.

"Alright, I'll go with you," Lisa answered. Pamela stared Lisa down as if she were waiting for an explanation from her. She knew Pamela liked him, or at least, that is what Pamela assumed. That was her best friend for crying out loud. She should have known.... Right?

"Wooooow, really Jerome? You're just going to hit on my best friend right in front of me, huh?"

Jerome laughed and Lisa got up to go with him. Lisa did not say a word to Pamela and that was Pamela's confirmation that Lisa had to know that she and Jerome had hung out in the past. Pamela just sat there in shock.

Ali came over and said, "You and that guy used to date, huh?" Pamela looked down as she twiddled her fingers. "I can't believe she just left with him in front of you like that. I'm sorry."

Pamela looked over at him and said, "Thank you, but we weren't dating. He flirted with me often and I just really liked him a lot. I am so sorry. Seeing my rection to that probably didn't make you feel good. I know you have strong feelings for me."

Ali comforted her and said, "It's okay. I know

93

that made you feel worse than I was feeling."

Pamela started to tear up. "I don't want to be with Jerome at all. It just hurt my feelings that they would do that in my face like that. I was just shocked, that's all," Pamela confessed.

Ali told her, "I know you have feelings for me, too, but I also know they are not as strong and that's okay. If you do not want to be in a relationship, being friends with you will still make me happy. I just want you to be happy." Pamela gave him a hug and kiss on the cheek. "Thank you, Ali. I do feel that we should just be friends. You're such a great guy, but my feelings aren't there."

Pamela looked down at her cell phone to check the time. It was time for her to catch the school bus back to the high school, where her mom could pick her up. The college was too far away from her mom's job, so she had to meet her at the high school instead. Pamela didn't have a car.

"Hey, do you need a ride?" Ali asked.

"No, it's okay. Lisa and I are the only people who ride this bus, and I don't want to leave her by herself," Pamela said.

Ali sat with Panela to wait for the bus to arrive. Once it pulled up, Pamela looked around but didn't see Lisa.

"Where is your friend?" Ali asked.

"I'm not sure," Pamela said.

A few moments later, Lisa walked out with Jerome and they both headed towards the parking lot.

"Hey Lisa, where are you going? Pamela asked.

"I'm not riding on the bus today; I'll talk to you later," Lisa said.

Pamela tried not to look hurt. She could not believe that Lisa had ditched her. This was going to be a long and lonely bus ride.

"Wow, I'm sorry Pamela. Are you sure you don't want to ride with me?" Ali offered again.

Pamela thanked him, but turned him down again. Ali hugged her and said he hoped she would feel better tomorrow. She slowly got on the bus and stared out the window the whole way back to the high school.

9 THE SMIRK AND THE HOT HEAD WITH POTENTIAL

It had been a month or so and Pamela still had not heard from Lisa. Pamela wanted to blame it all on Jerome but knew that she and Lisa were also just growing apart. Ali came in for his weekly visits and was okay with being just friends with Pamela. As Pamela and Ali chatted, Joe came strolling in with his chemistry book and the orange and blue bag with the shoulder strap. Ali knew Joe wanted to come over to talk to Pamela, so he went to watch some TV, to give Joe the space to come over. Joe walked over to Pamela while staring her down with a smirk on his face.

Ahhhh! Pamela loved his stare and could not help but blush as usual.

Joe said, "I'm sorry. I cannot help but stare at you. You are just so beautiful. I was just stopping by, before going home." Ms. Jones smirked, and Pamela smiled and waved goodbye as he left.

"I got next on the table!" said a male voice at the game room door.

It was Maurice. Ms. Jones rolled her eyes. Pamela looked over at her and said, "Here we go again." Maurice was one of the political guys who came into the game room. His pal, Otis, was already waiting for him at the ping pong table.

"They all know it's your turn, bro," Otis said sarcastically. Every time these two would play, they would argue and debate things that, by the end of game, turned into arguments over sensitive subjects, like politics and religion. It was annoying, but everyone was entertained and got a good laugh out of it.

Bing. Tap...Bing. Tap. Back and forth, the little white ball went. Maurice and Otis had been playing and having one of their discussions for about five minutes. The more intense the conversation got, the more spikes they each scored on one another.

"Okay, y'all, that's enough. Change the topic," Ms. Jones requested while waving her hand. Everyone started laughing and a few people stood up to discuss who was next in line to play.

"I want to play YOU!" Maurice said while pointing at Pamela.

"Who? Me?" Pamela asked.

"Yeah, you! You work here and I never see you

play," Maurice said. Ms. Jones gave Pamela the okay and Pamela grabbed one of the nice, thick paddles that had a green rubbery layer on both sides. "Are you ready?" Maurice asked.

Pamela nodded and they began to play. Most of the other players were tuned into this match because everyone wondered if Pamela had any skills on the ping pong table. It was rare that girls played ping pong in the game room. Typically, it was only guys playing, and the games always got super intense.

Bing. Tap...Bing. Tap...Bing. Tap...Bing. Tap. They both volleyed the ball for quite a while. Yogi, one of the guys who played daily, started jokingly taunting Maurice. "Okay, okay, just spike on her already. Quit going easy on her!"

Pamela agreed. "Yeah, stop going easy on me and let's do this!"

Maurice, perked up by Pamela's response, said, "Okay, let's do it then!"

The competition heated up and Pamela was still in the game. Of course, Maurice was winning and had spiked the ball several times, but Pamela never gave up. It was nearing the end of her shift and her adrenaline had started pumping. *I have to get a good spike in, before I go!* she thought. This ping pong game was feeling more like double dutch jump rope to her. She kept repeating to herself, *When can I get in there? Where can I spike the ball!?* Then...BAM! Pamela swung her paddle back and spiked the ball with gusto! The ball hit right at the corner of the table!

"Whoahhhhhhh!" the other players screamed. Pamela was so proud of herself. She laughed and slammed her paddle down.

"Lucky shot! But I am impressed," Maurice said as he chuckled. Pamela started blushing. "How about I take you out to lunch?" Maurice suggested.

"Hey, this is not the love connection. Get off the table, so we can play," Yogi said. Everyone started laughing.

Maurice and Pamela walked over to the desk. While Pamela clocked out, Maurice said, "So, about that lunch..."

Pamela looked at him and played hard to get. "I have to check my schedule, but I will let you know the next time I see you." Maurice smiled and walked out.

Ali walked over and smiled at Pamela before looking at his aunt.

"What!?" Pamela asked.

"You have all the guys coming after you, huh?" Ali said. Pamela started blushing. "So, who are you going to give a chance to? You clearly like both."

Pamela said, "Well, Joe is older than me and I don't know if I can trust him. I do not want any man trying to control me, just because I am young. Maurice is closer to my age, but he seems like he's a little hot-headed." Ali suggested that she should probably not date either of the guys and just take things slow. You would think he was trying to keep her all to himself, but that was not the case at all. He was trying to look out for her, and it turned out that he truly just wanted her to be happy.

"I don't know. I do like edgy guys though."

Over the next year, Maurice and Pamela grew closer and Joe had not been around. They had been on several dates and everyone marked them as the "opposites attract" couple. People kept joking about how Pamela must be a patient person to put up with Maurice's foolishness! Pamela would get annoyed with their discussions at times, but loved how he was able to carry on an interesting conversation.

One night, Maurice and Pamela were talking for hours over the phone. Pamela was asking probing questions and trying to figure out how serious the relationship was at this point. Maurice kept avoiding and dodging certain topics and turned the discussion into a joke. Pamela was not amused and grew silent over the next few minutes.

"Since you are not talking to me, I'm going to go eat dinner. *Olive Juice*," Maurice said. He said *olive juice* in a way that made it sound like he had said, *I love you*. Pamela perked up and asked, "Awwwww, did you just say you loved me?! Don't play with my emotions. Do you mean it?!"

Maurice burst into laughter and told her to calm down. RED FLAG.

"What's so funny?" Pamela asked.

"I was joking with you. I said 'olive juice', not 'I love you!'" he said. Pamela was so embarrassed. She told him how mean that was and hung up on him and went to bed.

"Paper down. Pencils down," the professor said. It was exam day.

Ugh, I was not prepared for this exam, Pamela thought. She let out a loud sigh and turned in her exam. Maurice's bad joke had distracted her so much that she had forgotten to study! She packed her stuff and slowly walked out of the classroom. She dragged her feet all the way to the game room. She opened the door and walked to the desk. Ms. Jones looked at her and smirked. Pamela looked over and saw a flower on the desk with a note.

"Who did this come from?" Pamela asked.

"Your little boyfriend," Ms. Jones said sarcastically. Pamela was trying not to smile, but she could not help it. She loved flowers; they were her weak spot. Ugh! She did not want to forgive him so easily.

"What did he do?" Ms. Jones asked.

"He was a jerk and played a mean joke on me over the phone last night," Pamela explained.

Pamela picked up the note. It read:

Pamela, I'm sorry about last night. You know I am always joking around, but I am sorry that I took it too far. I truly have feelings for you and to prove it, I would like you to meet my mom. She is coming to visit me tonight and I already told her about you. Please forgive me and I hope to see you tonight.

Love, Maurice

Pamela's eyes lit up and she felt all warm and fuzzy. Today was her long day. She had another couple of classes after her shift and she was not looking forward to going to them. She was too excited about this giant step that was about to happen tonight. *I have A's and B's in these next classes, so it won't hurt if I skip them just this once*, Pamela thought.

Two hours later, Pamela got ready to clock out. "Don't forget to come back and pick up your check at the end of the day," Ms. Jones reminded Pamela.

"I'm going home early today; I will pick it up tomorrow," Pamela said.

"But don't you have classes today? I know you are not skipping classes for your little boyfriend," Ms. Jones said jokingly.

"I know, I know, but I'm meeting his mom tonight and I need to be prepared!" Pamela said enthusiastically.

Ms. Jones smirked and shook her head. "Oooookay. Good luck with that."

Pamela's phone rang. She looked at the caller ID and saw that it was Maurice.

"Hello?" Pamela answered.

"Hey Pamela, did you get my surprise? I am so sorry about my joke last night!" he said.

"I did get it. Thank you. I cannot believe you want me to meet your mom. I can't wait to meet her."

Maurice breathed a sigh of relief and said, "I'm glad to hear that. I will see you in an hour. My mom will be here in two hours."

Pamela said, "Okay, see you soon." They both hung up and Pamela began to get ready. She went through a couple of outfits and could not seem to find the right one. She wanted to make sure she looked perfect for his mom. She must make a good impression. "Ma! Can you help me for a sec?" Pamela yelled from across the house.

Sarah walked in and was excited to help Pamela pick an outfit. She always wanted to pick out her clothes and accessories. She should have considered becoming a stylist. Sarah walked to the closet and quickly picked out the long sleeve, dark pink collared top, with dark blue jeans, and a clean pair of white sneakers. She searched for minimal-looking jewelry and a light lip gloss. "Okay, go look in the mirror," Sarah told Pamela.

She looked in the mirror and said, "This is perfect! Thanks Ma!" Pamela grabbed her purse and keys and hugged her mom goodbye.

"Good luck, hun! She's going to love you!" Sarah said.

"Thanks Ma! I love you!" Pamela said.

Maurice's apartment was about thirty minutes away from her mom's house. That was not a long trip, but her nerves made the trip feel like it took hours! She tried to take deep breaths and listen to music to relax her mind. It did not work; she was way too anxious! *What is wrong with me? Why am I so nervous about meeting his mom?* Pamela could not understand why she was feeling the way she was. Like the universe was trying to warn her about something. She finally arrived at his apartment and he greeted her at the door. They walked in and they both sat on the couch.

"My mom's plane arrived early, and she should be here any minute. Are you nervous?" Maurice asked.

"No, I'm excited to meet her!" Pamela said with a smile.

KNOCK. KNOCK. KNOCK. Pamela's heart sank and she had butterflies AND piranhas in her stomach.

"Hey, Mom!" Maurice greeted his mother.

"Hi, Maurice! How are you?" his mom said.

"I'm great. I want you to meet Pamela!"

His mom walked over to Pamela and gave her a huge hug. "Hi, sweetheart! My name is Gretta. It's so nice to finally meet you! My son won't stop talking about you."

That put Pamela at ease, and she said, "It is nice to meet you, too! Oh, he's been talking about me, huh?"

Pamela felt instantly comfortable with Gretta. While Pamela and Gretta had a quick chat, Maurice went off to answer his phone. When he returned, they all sat down at the small round table and talked for about forty-five minutes and then ate dinner together.

Through the dinner, Pamela still had an uneasy feeling in the pit of her stomach. She did not understand why, because she had gotten over her nerves about meeting Mrs. Gretta, who had put her at ease.

"Alright, son. I have to get going. There was an emergency at work. Pamela it was so wonderful meeting you, sweetheart. My son is lucky to have you!" Gretta said.

"Okay, Mom, thanks for the visit," Maurice said.

Pamela hugged Gretta and said, "It was so nice to meet you and I am lucky, too! Your son is great!"

Maurice walked his mom outside and Pamela went into his room. She wanted to surprise him with a fun night, especially after things had gone so well with meeting his mom.

Maurice came back in and looked for Pamela.

"I'm in here," Pamela called from the bedroom. Maurice walked in to see Pamela laying on his bed and giving him sultry, bedroom eyes.

"Pamela, we need to talk," he said in a cold

tone.

RED FLAG flying high. This was not the reaction Pamela was expecting.

"Ummm...my ex-girlfriend called me earlier and said she has big news," he continued. Pamela got silent and was trying to figure out what in the world that news could be!

His cell phone began to ring. "Ugh, that's her again. She won't stop calling me," Maurice said.

"Okay, well, you need to answer that and get this taken care of. Find out what she wants, so we can get back to our night," Pamela said sternly. Maurice took the call and walked out of the room. Pamela laid back down on the bed and tried to calm herself. After an entire hour, Maurice walked back into the room with a blank look on his face.

"So...what is it?" Pamela asked.

"Ummm...she told me she's pregnant. She's on her way now and wants to talk to me face to face," Maurice explained. Silence and blank stares were all that Pamela could give in that moment.

"Are you kidding me?!" she finally said. "She can't come right now. Tell her you guys can talk about this tomorrow. This is our night!"

Maurice looked down and said, "I can't. I have to talk to her." Pamela rushed out of the room and grabbed her purse and keys.

"Pamela, please don't leave," Maurice pleaded. Pamela walked out of the apartment to the parking lot. She got in the car and Maurice was not far behind. He stood by her car and asked her to stay.

"I can't do this. It's over," Pamela said with tears in her eyes. As she backed out, she saw a car pull up behind her. She pulled out of the parking spot and saw the driver was a young woman, and by the look on her face, it must have been his ex. Pamela screeched out of the parking lot and cried the whole way home.

10 THE GRIN AND THE YOUNG FLIRT

While most of her friends were enjoying the summer break with beach trips and movie nights, Pamela quit her job in the game room and took summer classes. Her guidance counselor from the community college, Mrs. Judy, had mentioned that if she took summer classes at the university, it could help her graduate earlier. Pamela's motto this time around changed to *sacrifice now and party later*. The good thing about summer classes was that they would help distract Pamela from the situation with Maurice.

"Crap, I'm lost," Pamela said while looking at the campus map. She kept walking through the roads, pausing every few steps. She looked down at the map again and just could not figure out where she was. *I'm going to be late to this orientation. Ugh!* she thought. She was starting to get sweaty and was feeling anxious. She did not want to leave a bad impression on the department head of the architectural program. Pamela looked around and there was no one in sight.

She saw Greek lettering on the fronts of houses and realized she was no longer on campus. *I'm really, really lost! What am I going to do!?* she thought. From the corner of her eye, she saw movement. She looked over and saw someone a few streets down.

"Hey, are you lost?" the person asked. Pamela was hesitant to answer. She did not want the stranger to know she was lost, but she was more worried about being late than about what this stranger could possibly do to her.

"Yes, I am trying to find the Architecture building. I have like five minutes to get there for orientation!" Pamela said to the stranger.

"It's not that far. Come back down this road, walk up two streets, and make a right. If you run, you can make it in like two minutes!" the stranger said. Pamela started power walking and said thank you to the stranger as she passed.

Pamela made it there a few minutes late. While panting hard, Pamela tried to look normal, while opening the door to the orientation. She was a little sweaty and could not catch her breath. "Hello, hard time finding the place?" The coordinator of the orientation tried to offer some comedic relief. Everyone chuckled and so did Pamela.

"Hi, I'm sorry I'm late. I got lost and ended up in the frat houses!" Pamela said. Everyone chuckled again. Orientation lasted about two hours and left Pamela feeling extremely excited about the architecture program and the classes she would be taking. Pamela got up and walked out the door. She pulled out her map and tried to find the bus stop. *Thank goodness, the bus stop is the next street over,* Pamela thought. There was no way she could get lost. She arrived at the bus stop and sat on the wood plank bench. She looked to the left and saw the bus number and the running schedule. She had to wait another twenty minutes until the next bus came along.

Pamela sighed and observed her surroundings. This campus was so beautiful and peaceful. There were so many trees and so much plant life intertwined with the hard brick, concrete, and glass buildings. Occasionally, she would hear engine noises with the hopes of it being the bus, but it was always just a car.

HONK. HONK. HONK. "Hey Pam! What's up girl!?"

Pamela looked up and smiled. "Oh, hey, Jeremy! How are you?"

Jeremy put his white truck in park and said, "I'm doing good! Are you waiting on the bus? Do you need a ride?"

Pamela stood up and said, "Yes, thank you so much! This bus is taking forever to get here." Pamela was shocked to see him there, of all places. The last time she saw him, they were at the college in the game room. He did not hang out there often, but the times he did, he had made a big impression on Pamela. She never entertained the thought of being with him, though, because he was younger than her. But there was something about him. He had swagger and confidence.

"So, are you taking classes here now? What's your major?" Jeremy asked.

"Yeah, I start tomorrow and I'm majoring in Architecture," Pamela said.

"Oh, wow, that's amazing!" Jeremy said.

There was a pause in the conversation and Pamela was able to hear music. She heard a familiar voice and realized it was him rapping. "Is that you rapping?" Pamela asked. He nodded his head to confirm. "I remember when you played one of your songs for me the first time, when we met in the game room! I didn't want to show it, but I was really impressed," Pamela added with a giggle.

"Oh yeah?" he asked. "I was trying to impress you, but you weren't giving me the time of day!"

"Look, you are a few years younger than me and I didn't think it would work out," she admitted. Jeremy held her hand and kissed it.

"You know you'll fall in love with me, right?" he said with a grin. Pamela rolled her eyes, shook her head, and smiled.

The car came to halt and Pamela realized that they had made it to her mom's house already.

"I have a performance tonight at the downtown

bar and I want you to come," Jeremy told her.

"No problem. I'd love to come out and show some support," she said.

"Here's my number. Give me a call when you are heading out that way. My two sisters will be there and can meet you inside," he told her as he winked. Pamela giggled, gave him a hug, and thanked him again for the ride. He drove off and beeped the horn as Pamela went inside.

"Hey, hun! Who was that?" Sarah asked her.

"Remember that younger guy from college who told me he raps? He was driving by the bus stop and gave me a ride home," Pamela said.

Sarah smirked and said, "So, you like him now?".

Pamela gave her mom the guilty look and giggled. "He has a performance tonight and his sisters will be there. I'm going to go meet them there in a few hours."

Sarah smiled and told her how nice of a gesture that was.

Pamela took a shower and tried to pick out clothes for that night. She wanted to look cool, but be comfortable at the same time, since she would be standing for a while. She looked in the closet and picked out a black lace top, black pants, a black leather jacket and black boots. She checked herself out in the mirror and was satisfied. She looked cool and did not look like she was trying too hard to impress him and his sisters.

Sarah looked at Pamela's outfit and said she looked great. "Thanks Ma. I'll see you later," Pamela said. She left the house and walked to her car. The drive was about fifteen minutes. She texted Jeremy to tell him she was there. He texted her back to say that his sisters were by the bar. Pamela sat in the car for a few minutes to try to calm down and prepare herself. She did not do well in crowds and did not do well with introductions.

"Hi ladies! I'm Pamela, Jeremy's friend!" Pamela yelled over the loud music.

"Oh, hey girl! It is nice to meet you!" his older sister, Lucy, said.

"Hey!" his younger sister, Kim, said, while hugging Pamela. The girls told her that his performance should start in a few minutes. They offered her a drink, but Pamela did not drink, so she politely turned them down with a smile. The lights dimmed and the bass of the music shook the windows. Jeremy walked onto the stage and started his show. Pamela and the sisters rushed into the crowd to support him.

They danced and recited all the words to his songs. Pamela felt so alive! This was the coolest thing she had ever been to and it was more fun because she knew the artist! It was also a bonus that his sisters were there, because she was able to meet some of his family in a laidback setting. But, this time, Pamela promised herself that she wouldn't read too much into meeting a guy's family.

"Hey, do you want to come over to our parents' house to hang with us for a little while? Our family had a barbeque earlier and are playing cards games now," Lucy asked Pamela.

Pamela quickly said, "Sure! Thank you!"

All three ladies went outside to the side of the building to meet up with Jeremy after the show.

"Nice job, bro!" Kim said.

"We invited Pamela to the house to hang out. Let's go!" Lucy said. The sisters went to their car and Jeremy walked Pamela to hers.

"Are you sure you want to come over? My sisters are known for putting people on the spot!" Jeremy said.

"I'm sure! It sounds fun. I like your sisters a lot and they made me feel very welcome!" Pamela said. They both got into their respective cars and Jeremy led the way. When they arrived at the house, Pamela could hear loud laughter and music. She saw several cars lined up along the street. *Everyone must still be here. I was not expecting there to be a lot of people.* Pamela was nervous and had no idea who she was going to meet now. She got out of her car and Jeremy led her to the door. They walked in and everyone crowded them.

"We heard you had a great show, son!"

Jeremy's mom said. Pamela's nerves were through the roof!

Oh no. I am about to meet his whole family. This is happening fast! Pamela thought.

"Hey, pretty girl! Come give me a hug! I'm Jeremy's mom, Sue," Jeremy's mom said. Pamela walked over and hugged her and was introduced to the rest of the family.

"We have heard some nice things about you, young lady." Jeremy's dad, Wilton, said.

"Okay, okay. Leave her alone, y'all," Jeremy said jokingly. He took her up to his room to show her his recording set up.

"This is so cool!" Pamela said. Jeremy sat down and showed her a little taste of how the equipment works. He searched for a track that he wrote for her and played it. "Okay, you listen to this and I will be right back," he told her.

She listened to the song and was impressed and touched. She could not stop smiling. *Creek!* The door slowly opened, and Lucy popped her head in.

"Hey, can I talk to you for a second?" she asked Pamela. Pamela had butterflies in her stomach because she knew what they were about to talk about.

"Of course!" she said.

"I see you are a nice girl, but I know that you are a few years older than my brother. Why are you

115

hanging out with him? Do you genuinely like him in that way?" Lucy asked out of concern.

"I really do like him. I know he is younger than me, but he does not act like it. We have fun and he treats me better than the guys my age! He has always been such a gentleman."

Lucy smiled, hugged her, and said, "Thank you for being honest with me. My little bro is going places and we are trying to make sure that the ladies aren't after him for the money or a shot at fame."

Pamela smiled and told her that she totally understood where she was coming from.

Jeremy walked back in to see both girls smiling and laughing. He was happy to see them hitting it off, because he knew his older sister was a direct and straight-to-the-point kind of person. Lucy left and Jeremy sat down at his desk to play another song. "What did you think of your song?" he asked her.

"I loved it! You are so creative with your words!" Pamela said. She looked down at her phone and noticed the time. "Sorry, I have to get going. I have class early in the morning."

Jeremy looked up and said okay. He led her out of the room and back into the living room.

"Are you leaving already?" Mr. Wilton asked.

"Yes, sir. I have class in the morning," Pamela said. She went around the room and gave everyone a hug and told them she enjoyed meeting them. Jeremy and Pamela walked to her car hand-in-hand.

"Thanks for coming to my show and for being so great with my family," he said.

"Anytime. I had fun," Pamela said. She got in the car, let the window down and they gave each other a kiss.

Pamela arrived home. "How did it go? Did you have a great time?" Sarah asked.

"It was so fun! I met his two sisters there and they were so nice. They invited me to hang out with them at their parents' house and I met some of his family. They were all so welcoming!"

Sarah smiled and said she was happy for her.

Pamela was feeling creative and wanted to do something for Jeremy as a thank you. Since he was a music producer and artist, she thought maybe she could try to write him a cute song! He wrote one for her, so it was only fitting that she did the same for him. *This shouldn't be too hard, since I write poetry all the time,* she thought. Since she could not sleep, she spent the next couple of hours writing the song and felt proud of herself. She sang the song to herself and thought he would love it. She was so excited that she did not want to wait until the next day to sing it to him, so she gave him a call.

RING. RING. RING. RING. RING. RING. No answer. *Okay, let me call him again and just leave it as a voice message,* she thought. She called him back and reached his voicemail. She began to sing softly. When she was done, she hung up and sat there for a minute. *Oh crap. I hope he doesn't think that I am trying to use him to get my song out there!* A chill went through her and her stomach started to hurt. It was too late now. She suddenly felt so embarrassed. All she could do was wait to see what he thought.

She did not hear from him for the next week. RED FLAG! *He must have thought I was trying to use him. Ugh! Now, he thinks I am a gold digger!* Pamela was not happy with herself. She just had to leave that message!

BEEP. BEEP. BEEP. She finally received a text from him which read: *Hey, I am sorry that I haven't reached out. I have been busy with my music. I will be around campus today and can give you a ride if you want.*

Pamela texted back: *No problem. I have been busy with my classes, too. Sure, a ride would be great, thanks.*

Pamela was relieved that he finally contacted her but was a little disappointed that he did not even mention the song. She got through her classes for the day and walked to the bus stop to wait for Jeremy. His truck pulled up and she went over to get in. She heard chatter and saw that he had a few friends in the truck with him. *Great*, she thought. She was wondering if they heard the song. She did not want them to pick on her.

"Y'all, this is my girl, Pamela," Jeremy said.

"What's up, Pam?" one of the guys said.

"It's nice to meet y'all," Pamela said. Jeremy blasted his music and drove off. As they cruised along, Pamela began to see Jeremy's true age show.

RED FLAG! The conversations that he and his friends were having were telling. She was able to pick up on some bad habits he had and the kind of activities he was into. *Okay, this is not going to work out,* Pamela thought to herself. She felt embarrassed again and felt so old suddenly. Driving through town, she was hoping no one she knew saw her in the truck. She was worried people would think that she could not get a guy her age.

As they approached her mom's house, she politely asked Jeremy to turn his music down. He turned it down and slowed near the house.

"Thank you so much and it was nice to meet y'all," Pamela said sweetly.

"You, too!" the guys said.

"I'll call you later," Jeremy added.

Pamela contemplated how she was going to let him down gently that night. She wanted to just cut it off before things went too far. She decided to give him a call and not wait on him. She wanted to end this tonight and did not want to risk him not calling for a week again.

RING. RING. RING. "Hello?"

Pamela sighed and said, "Hey, Jeremy. Can we

talk?"

Jeremy paused then said, "I know where this is going and it's okay."

Pamela felt relieved. She said, "I'm sorry, I just feel that we are in different places in our lives and we would be better off as just friends."

Jeremy agreed and was super cool about it. "You're such a great girl and I want you in my life in any way I can," he said with a giggle.

"Thanks for understanding. I have to get up early for class. Have a good night," Pamela said. They both hung up and she went to bed feeling at peace.

11 THE GRIN AND THE MATURE CRUSH

The next semester had become more difficult than the first and Pamela was feeling lonelier than ever. She had tried to socialize and make new friends last semester, but it was hard for her. The workload was so intense, and she was not catching onto things as quickly as everyone else. She did not have the luxury of getting off track with her class projects, so she constantly turned down lunch invites from her classmates. While some of her classmates procrastinated during the day then pulled all-nighters to finish them, Pamela finished her projects ahead of time.

"You're late and that is unacceptable. You have missed the first assignment and will need to get with one of the other students to catch up," her new professor, Mrs. Rivers, said in front of the entire class. Pamela had gotten her schedule mixed up with her previous one and was late to class and had missed most of it.

"I'm so sorry. It will never happen again," Pamela promised. Mrs. Rivers gave her a look of disapproval and continued with the instructions for the new project that was due the next morning. *Great, now I have two major assignments due in the morning*, Pamela thought. Her classmate, Amy, whispered to her and said that she would help her catch up on what she missed.

It was time for a break and Pamela stepped out of the studio classroom to get some fresh air. She felt even more alone but kept a brave face. A rush of people came out of the classroom next to her and she moved out of the way. As she looked over, there was a guy standing there with his back towards her, talking to his classmate. *He looks familiar and I have seen that orange and blue over the shoulder bag before,* she thought. He turned around to leave and Pamela realized it was Joe from the game room! She was so excited and felt such relief to see a familiar face—especially his! He turned toward her, did a double take, and recognized Pamela.

"It is so great to see you, Pam! It's been a while!" Joe hugged Pamela tightly.

"You have no idea how good it is to see you right now! Are you taking classes in the Architecture building, too!?" she asked.

"Yes, I'm taking this class twice a week. What's

wrong?" Joe asked.

"I've been having a rough day. It's a long story," she explained with a sigh. "I have two projects due in the morning. I better go back in and start working on them."

"Okay, I hope to see you around and hope your day goes better!" Joe said. He hugged her again and walked away. Pamela walked back into the studio classroom and sat in silence to try to focus. As the other students trickled back into the studio, she began to work.

She flew through the first project, but this second one was tough. She had to duplicate a drawing of a home of a famous architect. There were so many details and it had to be hand drawn as a mirror image. It took hours for her to get not even a third of the project done. *There is no way I can finish this on time,* she thought. Pamela was feeling defeated. This was not a good start to the semester. Not only was she late, but she was now going to get an incomplete grade on her project. She looked around and saw that everyone else was in the same predicament as her. No one could figure out how to do this in time. She felt better knowing that they were all in this together. This could be a bonding moment and hopefully lead to making some friends.

"Have you figured it out?" Bill asked Pamela.

"No, not yet. This is really hard. It's impossible to finish by tomorrow," Pamela said softly.

An hour went by and the heavy metal door swung open. "How's it going? Have you guys finished the project yet?" a male voice said. It was their professor's teaching assistant, Max. Everyone shook their heads while huffing and puffing. Seeing how down everyone was, Max offered to help. "There is a trick that you can use to finish the project. Just open the drawing in the editing program, mirror it, print it out and then trace it! We used this trick when I took this class," Max said.

While everyone else was waiting for Max to make the printouts for them, Pamela said, "I don't know about this, you guys. I'm not sure we can do it this way."

Her classmate, Stephanie, said, "The TA said his class got away with it, so I'm definitely doing it." A few others muttered their agreement. Pamela felt alone again. The TA came back in and handed out a few copies. He went around and showed them how to do the project. Pamela sat at her desk and continued trying to figure it out on her own. One by one, the other students completed the project and left. Max was the only one remaining and walked over to Pamela.

"Why won't you just trace it? You won't finish in time," he said.

"I just can't do it. I have a bad feeling about it," Pamela replied. He shrugged and wished her luck.

The next day, Pamela dragged her feet the whole way to class. She hadn't completed the project and she was not looking forward to Mrs. Rivers chewing her out about it.

"Okay, everyone, pin up your work and we will review them one at a time," Mrs. Rivers said when the time came to present projects. Each person pinned up their work and Pamela was the last to do it. She was pouting and silent because she only completed about half of the drawing. She was so nervous and knew that the professor was going to embarrass her in front of the whole class. Pamela did not want to be labeled a bad student. One by one, each person gave a BS explanation of how they were able to complete the drawing. The more Pamela heard the bogus explanations, the more pissed she became. She wanted so badly to tell Mrs. Rivers that the TA helped the others cheat on the assignment.

"I see most of you were able to complete the project. Pamela, you did not complete it. Can you explain your process for working on the drawing?" Mrs. Rivers asked. Pamela slowly walked up to her drawing with dread. While fighting back tears, she explained how she tried to do the drawing.

"I am disappointed in this class. All of you owe me and Pamela an apology. This project can't realistically be completed in the time frame that I gave, so, since you all completed it, I know you cheated. I am sure you all made Pamela feel bad for being the only one who didn't complete the assignment and that is not fair to her," Mrs. Rivers confessed.

Everyone looked down at the floor and grew silent. Moments passed and a few people offered their apologies. Pamela was in shock. After all that fuss, the professor saw right through the other students' crap. She was so happy that Mrs. Rivers finally recognized her for the true student she was, an honest student who wanted to do well in the class. Everyone sat back down at their desks and Pamela went outside for a short break.

"Hey Pam! How is class going today? Did you finish your project?" Pamela looked over and saw Joe! She sighed and told him what happened. Mid-sentence, Joe leaned in and kissed Pamela! She was caught off guard. That kiss was so gentle, passionate, and made her feel so light on her feet suddenly.

"I have to go," Joe said. He slipped her a letter and walked away. Pamela felt better and was excited to read the letter. She decided to read it later that night, so she could focus on her classes for the rest of the day.

I think I am going to give him a chance. Pamela wrote to Rod, her childhood friend from elementary school. They had become good friends and had been writing each other letters and messaging online for years now, ever since he joined the army and was stationed in Iraq.

Isn't he the guy that was way older than you? I thought you didn't want to date him? What changed? he wrote back.

He kissed me and wrote me a letter today. I think he is serious about me and he has always been nice and respectful to me, she wrote.

Just be careful. Do not make it too easy for him. Get to know him a little better first, Rod wrote. *I have to go. I can't chat past my curfew or my sergeant will make us do drills all night! Let's video chat next week. Our equipment is finally fixed.*

Okay, sounds like a plan. See you then, Pamela wrote.

She closed her laptop and took out the letter. She took a deep breath and opened it. The letter read:

Hey Pamela. Through our time in college, I kept my distance. I know we have years between us, but I truly have feelings for you. I tried to forget about you after you graduated, but after seeing you yesterday, I can't hide from my feelings. I am in a complicated relationship right now, but I just cannot stay away from you. I need a little time to figure out if she and I will work out or not, but I hope you can wait for me. I want to see where this goes. Please keep an open mind.

Love, Joe.

Pamela sat there, dumbfounded. *Seriously?!* she thought. She was no stranger to disappointment when it came to guys, but this one took the cake. She went from feeling like he was her hero, saving her from loneliness at school, to a guy who made her feel like a fool. *Does he really think this is okay? He kissed me and he has a girlfriend. Not cool*, she thought. *But, that kiss...OMG.*

A week passed and she had not seen Joe at the

Architecture building. After class, she walked across campus to go to the computer lab. She needed to use a certain computer program for her team project that was only available there. She entered the large room filled with computers. Aisle by aisle, she walked to find an empty seat. As she walked through row seven, she heard a male voice whisper, "Hey beautiful, over here."

She slowly turned her head to look but was trying to not look obvious. It was Joe. He was there, working on an assignment with a partner from class. Pamela walked over and hugged him, and he gave her a friendly peck on the cheek. They clearly could not have the much-needed conversation there, so Pamela just continued to find a spot to work. A couple hours passed, and she completed all she could for that day. She looked up and saw that Joe had already left. There was no telling when she would see him next.

She had been debating whether she should give him a chance or not. It was not fair to her that he put her in this situation. She thought about distancing herself from him and wanted to ignore him, but randomly seeing him around campus brought her so much comfort and joy. She did not want to give that up. As long as she was friendly and did not cross any lines, she felt okay with keeping their friendship. But she knew she had to set him straight and let him know that until he was officially single, they could not kiss or talk about a possible relationship. The next day was Thursday and she knew she would see him at the Architecture building. All night she rehearsed what she was going to say to him. She wanted to be firm, yet gentle enough that he would still want to talk to her when they crossed paths on campus.

The next day, Pamela was exhausted. She was up all night and only got a couple hours of sleep. She got through her first class okay but was lagging in the next class. It was time. Class was about to pause for a break, and she was ready to see Joe. She walked outside and leaned against the balcony railing to people watch for a bit. Pamela felt a gentle tap on her shoulder and Joe was there. He grabbed her and started singing to her.

That's not fair! He knows I melt every time I hear his voice! she thought. When he finished, she had to quickly shake it off. She had to focus on what she had to tell him. Before she could get a word out, he told her he was going to miss her. Pamela was so confused.

"What are you talking about?" she asked.

"I'm graduating next week and I'm moving to Atlanta."

Pamela was floored! She got a little teary-eyed and looked down. Joe held her hand and said, "I know we never got the chance to talk about my letter, but now things have changed. My girlfriend and I have worked things out. We are moving there together."

Pamela tried to smile and said, "I'm genuinely happy for you guys and I hope it works out. I really do." Joe hugged her and walked away. *Great, now I'm all alone again. I really need to be more social and make some new friends*, she thought.

12 THE GRIN AND THE SOLDIER WITH POTENTIAL

BLEEP. BLEEP. BLEEP. The video messenger started ringing.

"Hey girl!" Rod said as he waved at the camera. Pamela looked at her screen and saw Rod was laying down on his camo-covered cot inside of a large, beige tent.

"Hey you! How are you? Are you still doing okay over there?" she asked.

"Things are going alright, but I'm really homesick," he admitted.

"I'm sorry, Rod. I wish I could help," Pamela sweetly said.

"But you are helping! The letters that you send

me make me feel at home. I'm so thankful that you've kept in touch with me for all of this time!" he said. "I have good news!" Pamela looked curious and asked what the news was. "I'm coming home for a visit in two days!" Rod yelled with excitement.

"OMG! That is so great! I cannot wait to see you!" Pamela exclaimed.

"I can't wait to see you, too!" Rod said with a huge smile.

"Chow time!" Rod's sergeant announced.

"I have to go, but I will see you soon!" He quickly closed the laptop. Pamela was so excited and kept thinking of how great it would be to finally see and hug him after all these years! She had not physically been in his presence since middle school! She was picturing this huge reunion with warm embraces with passionate kisses.

It felt like Christmas! The next two days went by so slowly. Pamela had not heard from Rod yet and was hoping that things had gone as planned. With her dad being in the military her whole life, she knew how plans could change at the drop of a hat. *I hope they did not cancel his vacation time. I hope he is okay; I hope nothing happened out there!* Pamela thought.

"Ouch!" Pamela said. She had burned herself on the hot oil basket that was holding the fries.

"Are you okay!?" her manager asked. Pamela had started a campus job at a burger joint a few days prior.

"Yes, I am fine. But I think I burned myself." The manager led her to the first aid kit, and they took care of her wrist.

"Okay, you're going to work on milkshakes for the rest of the week," her manger said. Pamela had burnt herself a couple times already and her manger had to put a stop to it.

Within the next hour, her shift was over. Her cell phone had a few text notifications; she was not allowed to use her phone while she was working. She clocked out and went outside to check her messages.

I'm home! I am going to visit a few friends first, then I will be able to see you, Rod's text read.

Pamela felt relieved and happy. She was glad he had made it home safely. She texted him back to ask him what time he thought they could meet up. She had to figure out if she had time to go to the studio to work on an assignment or if she should just hang out at the food court.

I should only be an hour or two. Where should I meet you? he wrote.

I just got off work, so I will be here at the food court on campus. Just call me and I can direct you to where I am when you get here, she wrote back. She looked down at her work uniform and started debating whether she needed to change or not. She wanted everything to be perfect for their reunion and did not want to smell like fast food when she hugged him. She did not want to wait any longer to see him than she needed to, so she made the decision to just stay put and maybe air herself out outside, on the balcony.

An hour went by and then another. Pamela looked down at her phone and did not see a text or missed phone call. *Where is he?* she wondered. *If I were him, I would rush here to see me. He is probably enjoying his friends. I must be fair. They have not seen him in years either!*

Another thirty-five minutes passed and, finally, she received a text message from him.

I'm on campus. Where are you at?

It was too long to text, so she decided to call him. She told him how excited she was to finally see him and directed him to her location. They both stayed on the phone until she spotted him from afar. "I'm on the balcony. Look up," Pamela said. He waved and made his way up the wide concrete stairs. He worked his way through the crowd and gave her a big hug.

"You're so tall!" Pamela joked. "Back in middle school, I was taller than you!"

"It's good to finally see you," he said softly. There were a few moments of awkward silence. Pamela was feeling underwhelmed suddenly. She had pictured this amazing moment and it turned out to be a flop. He was not showing a lot of emotion.

RED FLAG. *Maybe he is just being shy,* she

thought.

"Do you want to go somewhere and hang out for a bit?" he asked her.

"Sure," Pamela said. They walked over to his car and got in. More awkward silence. He was still not very talkative, and Pamela did not know what to say. She was feeling a little shy herself. They drove around for a few minutes and arrived at a house.

"Where are we?" Pamela asked.

"This is my aunt's house. She wanted to see me tonight."

Pamela felt nervous. *Okay, he wants me to meet his family. That is a good sign. Maybe he was just nervous about this and that is why he has been shy and quiet,* she thought.

They got out of the car and walked up to the door. He opened the door and they both walked in to find his aunt sitting on the recliner.

"Hola, mi amor!" she said as she ran up to hug him.

"Hola, Tía" he said to her. Pamela stood awkwardly near the TV, waiting for him to introduce her to his aunt.

"Who is this pretty lady?" his aunt asked.

"This is Pamela," he said. "Pamela, this is my aunt, Rosa."

134

Pamela walked up to her to shake her hand. "It's nice to meet you!"

Rosa ignored the hand gesture and reached out for a hug. Rod and his aunt caught up for a few minutes. "We have to go, Tía. I will see you tomorrow. I have to take Pamela home," he explained. Rosa told Pamela that she was glad to meet her and glad that Rod had found a sweet girl. Pamela smiled and blushed a little. *Wow, this is getting real. He must really like me to bring me around his family and she likes me already,* she thought.

"She's so nice! I like her," Pamela said to Rod.

"Yeah, she's great," he said. They both walked to the car and got in. On the way to Pamela's mom's house, the conversation got better. They talked about his plans for vacation and what his schedule looked like before he had to go back to Iraq. They arrived at the house and parked in the driveway. Pamela did not want to go in yet, so she tried to keep the conversation going by asking about his time during his deployment. There were several stories that he had not told her during their times writing each other, so there was plenty to talk about.

Hours went by and it was getting late. "I have to get going. I still have some people that I need to see," Rod said.

"Okay. Thanks for a great night and I'm so happy that I got the chance to hang out with you," Pamela said. She awkwardly sat in the car for a few seconds too long. She was waiting for him to kiss her. He sat there and was looking around. He did not try to hug her or kiss her.

RED FLAG.

"Okay, I guess I will talk to you tomorrow," Pamela said, and she got out of the car.

He backed out, waved at her, and drove off. Pamela went inside and told her mom about her night. She went into her room and replayed the night in her head. She was so confused. Did Rod like her or not? Why would he introduce her to his aunt if he was not feeling serious about her? About ten minutes later, she received a long text from Rod. It read, *Hey Pamela. I am sorry, but I cannot see you again. I think you have feelings for me and want to be more than friends, but I do not feel the same way. I thank you for being there for me and I hope that we can still be friends from afar.*

Pamela's mouth dropped. She went to her mom's room and looked at her with the most confused look on her face.

"What's wrong, hun?" Sarah asked.

"Rod just texted me and said that he didn't want to hang out with me anymore. He said he just wants to be friends and that he doesn't like me in that way!" Pamela explained.

"Why would he introduce you to his aunt then? That doesn't make any sense," Sarah said.

"I don't know. I thought guys only introduced you to family when they were interested in you," Pamela said sadly. "After all of the time I spent being there for him and supporting him, I thought we were growing into something more than just friends."

Sarah comforted Pamela and told her to not let him get her down and that one day he would realize the mistake he just made.

Four days passed and Pamela had not heard from Rod at all. She was over it and was no longer hurt, but she was still trying to figure out what happened. *Maybe I was reading too much into our relationship? Maybe this was just a friendship the whole time and nothing more? How embarrassing,* she thought.

BING. She received a text message. *This better not be him.* she thought, even though she secretly hoped he would text her again.

She looked down at her phone and read his text. *It read: Hey Pamela. I am sorry again for how I acted that night. I was tipsy from hanging with my friends before I came to see you...*

Pamela paused reading and breathed a sigh of relief. She had butterflies in her stomach and thought, *Thank goodness. Something had to be going on with him to act that way. We still have a chance!* But then she thought, *Wait...he was tipsy and drove!? I can't be with a guy that would drive under the influence like that!*

She continued reading the text. *I didn't mean to give you mixed signals and I hope that you will still be my friend. When I go back to Iraq, I would love it if we could still keep in touch.*

Pamela let out a long and pitiful sigh. She swore that she would forget these guys and just focus on school. After a while, she got used to being alone. Every day she went to class, surrounded by strangers, and just kept to herself. To keep herself from thinking about guys at all, she kept a strict schedule down to the minute and it was beginning to become a bit obsessive.

"Pamela, are you okay? You seem stressed," her classmate, Shannon, said.

"I'm okay, thank you," Pamela replied.

"I'm here if you need someone to talk to!" Shannon said kindly.

Pamela smiled and said thank you. Shannon was someone she had met the day of orientation in the Architecture building and they had hit it off. They could have been great friends by now if Pamela had not been so boy crazy. Throughout the semester, Shannon had made several attempts to get closer to Pamela, but Pamela always kept to herself. Now that Pamela took her focus off guys, she was willing to work on being more social.

13 THE SMILE AND THE FLIRT WITH POTENTIAL

It was Pamela's final semester at the university, and she could not be prouder of herself. She was doing better in her classes and even made a few friends! Shannon had become Pamela's rock throughout the year. Whenever Pamela would have a meltdown about a project or fell back into her obsession with keeping a tight schedule, Shannon was there to help her through it.

"Are you ready for the final project?" Shannon asked Pamela.

"I guess so. This is going to be a long one. I cannot believe that we are spending an entire semester on one project," Pamela said with a concerned tone. There was an amazing internship opening at an Architecture firm that she was interested in going after. She was worried that if she got the job, it would interfere with her project. But, if she didn't get a good internship, it would make it harder for her to find a job after she graduated. "Hello? Earth to Pamela!" Shannon shouted. Pamela laughed and they both walked into the studio.

At the end of class, there was time to spare before the next class. "I'm meeting a couple of friends at the café; do you want to come along?" Shannon asked Pamela.

"Sure, I'd like that," Pamela said. They walked over to the café. Pamela had not been to this one before. She usually did not go near this area of campus. She hung out for a little while but left early to go back to the part of campus where her next class was. It was a long walk, but Pamela enjoyed it. It was sunny with clear skies and the wind was blowing gently. As Pamela strolled along, she passed by the administrative building. It was all brick with grand stairs that led to the wide double door entry.

"Pamela, is that you!?" a male voice said. Pamela looked up. *It was Vance!*

"It has been so long! Crazy running into you here of all places! The last time we were here together was when we were in that summer program," Pamela said.

"I'm in a rush to get somewhere, but here is my number. I would love to catch up!" Vance said. He gave Pamela his number, took her number, and rushed away.

The universe made me go to the café with

Shannon for a reason! If I had not come, I would not have seen Vance! This was meant to be, Pamela thought. She had butterflies in her stomach. She forced herself to block them out for the rest of the day, so she could focus on her classes. She had to remind herself that she had promised she would not get boy crazy. This was her last semester, and she could not get distracted now. She walked to class and was able to concentrate. The class seemed to pass quickly, and it was time for her to head home. She took out her phone and began to search for Vance's name in her list of contacts.

"Stop it!" Pamela said to herself. She did not want to seem too eager and wanted to wait to see if he would call her first. If he did, then maybe that would mean that he really liked her. Not wanting to read too much into it, Pamela tried to avoid getting too excited about his call.

Pamela was now home and there was still no word from Vance. Pamela pulled out her phone and began to search for his name again. "No!" Pamela said to herself. She was trying so hard not to call him first. She did not want to look desperate. She put her phone down and rolled over in her bed. She was about to take a nap, but then her phone rang.

Pamela jumped up and grabbed her phone. She looked down at the caller ID and saw that it was Vance! She let the phone ring a couple of times, so it didn't look like she was sitting there, waiting for his call.

"Hello?" Pamela said.

"Hey Pamela, it's Vance!"

Pamela paused and said, "Oh, hi! How are you?"

"I'm great, thanks. It was so nice running into you today. I was so happy to see you!" he said with excitement. They talked for a couple hours and the conversation was light and fun. "Hey, I had a little crush on you when we were in that summer program," Vance eventually confessed.

Pamela tried not to show her excitement. "Oh yeah? Why didn't you tell me at the time?" she asked.

"There were a lot of other guys who liked you and I wasn't sure that you liked me in that way, so I just backed off," he said.

"That is unfortunate. I had a crush on you, too. I was always wishing that you would flirt with me," Pamela confessed.

Vance laughed and said, "Aw man, I wish I would have known that!" Pamela tried not to read too much into that comment. "Can I come by a little later tonight? I would like to come see you before I drive back." He lived in Tampa and was only in Jacksonville to visit his baby daughter.

"Sure, I would like that," Pamela said. She heard laughing and roughhousing in the background. "What is going on over there?"

"I am hanging with the boys. I have to go,"

Vance said.

BEEP. (Silence).

"Hello?" Pamela said. *Did he just hang up on me?* RED FLAG. An hour went by and no word from Vance. This was very inconvenient. Was he coming over or not? If not, Pamela would be able to get ready for bed and get comfortable. She almost called him but didn't want to be pushy.

DING. Pamela looked down at her phone. It was her current best friend, Mitch. She was happy to hear from him but was disappointed that it was not Vance.

Hey bestie, want to hang out tonight? Mitch wrote.

Not tonight, I might be hanging with an old friend tonight. I am waiting on him to tell me what time he is coming by, Pamela texted back.

Here you go again, Pam... Mitch wrote. He was always trying to save her from herself when it came to dating, but she was so hardheaded! Through the years, Mitch had slowly turned into her best friend as she and Lisa had grown apart. Lisa had been dating an older guy and spent less and less time with Pamela as time went on.

I know, I know. Lol, Pamela wrote back.

BING. Pamela received another text. She looked down and saw that it was Vance...finally! It was 11 p.m. and he was just now getting back to her. Pamela fought with herself. She knew she needed to tell him to forget about tonight, but on the other hand, she did not want him to change his mind about hanging out with her. She read his text: *I am sorry about earlier. One of my friends took my phone and hung up as a joke. Can I come over?*

Pamela texted back and told him he could come over now, but that he could not stay long. It took about thirty-two minutes for him to arrive.

BING. I'm here, his text read. Pamela flew to the door, told her mom that a friend was passing by and went outside. He got out of his car as she walked toward it. They hugged each other and sat on the trunk of the car. Hours went by and Pamela's mom, Sarah, went outside to check on Pamela before she went to bed.

"Are you okay?" Sarah asked.

"I'm fine. I'm still out here with my friend, Vance," Pamela said.

"Hello, I'm Vance. It is nice to meet you."

Sarah said hello, introduced herself, and went back inside to give them their privacy.

More hours passed. Both Pamela and Vance looked down at their phones and saw that it was almost 4 a.m.! They had been talking for hours! Pamela was pleasantly shocked that they were able to talk for so long. She took that as a sign of good communication, which was important in a relationship. But the conversation was all about him, so I guess that made it

144

easy for him.

RED FLAG.

"I had a great time talking to you, Pam. I must get going, though. I'm driving back to Tampa in the morning," Vance said. They jumped down from the car and gave each other a hug.

"Thanks for coming to visit and drive safe. Please let me know when you make it there," Pamela said.

"No problem. I had a great time," Vance said. He got into the car and drove off. Pamela went back inside. Her mom was asleep, so she tip-toed back to her room.

The next morning, Pamela looked down at her phone. No text messages and no missed calls. "Did you make it?" she texted him. No response all day. *I hope he is okay,* she thought.

At around 10 p.m. she finally got a text message from him. *I am okay. I wish I could see you this weekend.*

Pamela blushed and tried to figure out how to respond to that. She did not want to say yes too quickly, but also did not want to give him the impression that she did not want to see him. *I would like that. I can drive to Tampa tomorrow morning, so we can spend the day hanging out. I would love to get out of the city and get a break from working on my project,* she wrote.

145

Sounds great. I will see you tomorrow then, Vance replied. Pamela was excited. This was her first car trip out of town alone and she was a little nervous. Tampa was not that crazy of a drive from Jacksonville but driving to an unfamiliar place was a little scary for her. She scraped up some change for the tolls, packed a few things in her purse and placed everything next to the door. She checked the weather forecast for the next day and saw that it might rain, but she refused to let a little rain stop her. *Maybe I will get lucky and it will pass. Since I am leaving early in the morning, I may get there before it rains!* Pamela thought. She told her mom about her plans, so someone would know where she was.

Of course, Pamela did not get any sleep that night and she woke up feeling surprisingly perky. She was not as exhausted as she should have been. She double checked her purse, recounted her change, and input his address in the maps app on her cell phone.

"Be safe on the road, hun. I love you and have fun," Sarah told Pamela. Pamela told her she loved her too and off she went! She grabbed her stuff and got into the car. The gas was a little low, so she stopped at the gas station first. After pumping her gas, she sent Vance a quick text to tell him that she was on her way.

He texted back, *Okay, great. See you soon.*

Pamela jumped back in the car and started driving towards the interstate. Pamela did not stop once. She was adamant about getting there as quickly as possible. Hours went by and she finally arrived in

Tampa. It was already overcast, and it looked like it was about to start raining. *I made it just in time!* Pamela thought. She texted Vance to say that she was minutes away from his house. When she arrived, he walked out and greeted her with a big hug.

"I am glad you made it here okay and it looks like you barely beat the rain," he said with a smile.

Pamela smiled and said, "Yeah, the drive was nice."

It rained for a couple hours and they spent the time talking and binge-watching a cooking show. Once the rain let up, Vance turned to Pamela and asked if she was hungry. There was a cool place to eat that he wanted to take her to. They headed to his car. The drive was only a few minutes before they pulled up to the café.

Pamela said, "This looks like a nice place. We have one of these restaurants in Jacksonville, but I've never been before."

They got out of the car and walked to the entrance. He opened the door for her, and they walked in. Vance put his order in and then Pamela did the same. The waitress led them to a light wooden table with benches where they sat. Pamela looked around at the décor. There were palm trees, paper lanterns, and flowers, and overhead, the roof looked like a hut.

"This place is so fun and relaxing!" Pamela said. Vance agreed and told her that a lot of students went there in between classes.

The food arrived and they both devoured it. It was so good! "I haven't had food this great in a long time!" Pamela said. She was not sure if the food was THAT great, or if it just seemed that way, because she was so excited to be there with Vance.

"Can I help you with anything else?" the waitress asked.

"No, we're okay. Can you please bring separate checks?" Vance said.

"Sure, not a problem. I will be right back," the waitress said. Pamela tried not to look disappointed, because she was trying not to make a big deal out of paying for half. This seemed to be the norm nowadays, but she was still struggling with it.

Vance searched his pockets for his wallet.

"Ummm. I'm sorry, I think I left my wallet at home. Oh well, it is what it is. Can you pay for us both and I will pay you back later?" Vance asked.

RED FLAG!

Pamela once again tried not to show her disappointment. She was already trying to be cool about paying for half, but now she had to pay for it all?

"Sure, no problem," Pamela said.

Pamela paid and then they made their way out of the restaurant. On the drive back to his house, they could see that the clouds were rolling in again.

"I better get back on the road," Pamela said in a monotone voice.

Vance looked a little sad and asked why she was leaving so soon. "If you're worried about the rain, you can stay a little longer, until it passes."

Pamela agreed and they went inside. They both checked the weather on their phones and saw that the skies should clear up in the next hour or two. They sat on the couch and started watching the cooking show again. After three hours, the weather seemed okay.

"I have to get going. It's finally nice outside again," Pamela said. She gathered her purse and jacket and they both walked to her car.

"I had fun! Thanks for visiting me. Come back again if you ever need a break from your projects!" Vance told her.

"I had fun too. Thanks for having me." Pamela stood awkwardly, waiting for him to kiss her. He started to walk away and then she got into her car. She was confused and wondered why he hadn't kissed her. *Maybe he is just being a gentleman?* she thought. The whole drive home, she replayed their time together in her mind.

"How did it go?" Sarah asked Pamela when she arrived back home.

"It was fun! We watched TV and he took me to

a great café for lunch. The food was amazing!" Pamela said. She walked to her room and texted Vance to let him know that she made it safely.

I am glad to hear that, Vance texted back.

Later that night, Pamela was trying to think of a gift to make for Vance. Clearly, she did not learn her lesson from back in high school when she made those *pretty eyes* pants for Brian. She tried to think of something that could be useful. She thought of a hat, but he didn't seem to wear them much. Then, she thought of a drawstring backpack. *Yes! He uses those a lot!* Pamela thought. She went digging through her drawers to find materials. She took out some beige fabric and her sewing machine.

She completed the construction of the bag and now had to figure out how to personalize it. She wanted it to be simple, but impressive. She remembered a saying that he always said. It was his favorite answer to anything that didn't go as planned—*it is what it is*. She spent hours working on the bag. She hand-embroidered the saying and his initials onto the fabric. She used his favorite colors for the lettering and outlined them in black, so the letters could pop. When she was done, she took a picture of it. She wanted to surprise him with it the next time he was in town, but could not wait! She texted him the picture.

That is awesome! You did that for me? Vance texted back.

I sure did! I wanted to make this as a thank you

for such a great time. The next time we see each other, I can give it to you, she wrote.

I should be in town this weekend, so I can swing by to pick it up, he replied. Pamela texted back, saying that sounded good and that she could not wait to see him.

That Sunday afternoon, Vance texted Pamela to tell her he was a few minutes away. She grabbed his bag and went outside to sit in the rocking chair on the front patio. He pulled up and she walked towards the car. He got out and gave her a hug. He told her that he could not stay long because he had to drop his daughter off at her mother's house.

"She's in the car?" Pamela asked. Vance opened the door and allowed Pamela to see her. Pamela said hi and told her she was so beautiful. His daughter, barely a toddler, tried to smile, but was so exhausted from the day. "Okay, here is your bag. I hope you like it," Pamela said.

He looked it over and appeared very touched. "This is so great, thank you!" he told her. He closed the back-passenger door and walked around to the driver's side. No hug and no kiss goodbye.

RED FLAG.

"I have to go. Thank you again!" he said.

"You're very welcome. Have a safe drive home!" she said. As Pamela walked back towards the patio, she was so happy that he liked the bag. She wanted him to kiss her and wondered why he didn't. *Maybe he did not want to confuse his daughter. She would not understand why her daddy was kissing someone who was not her mom,* Pamela thought.

Months passed and Pamela had visited Vance in Tampa quite a few times. It could be sunny or rainy, night or day—it did not matter to her anymore. It was worth it to see him. But he never went out of his way to visit her and only offered to pay for gas and tolls like once or twice. If he did stop by, it was just a drive by visit while he was visiting other people.

RED FLAG. Pamela had let this go on for too long. *Why is he not trying to be with me officially?* It was time for a talk. The next time she went to visit him, she let him know how she was feeling.

"I understand what you are feeling, but I do not think we would work out. We are in different places in our lives. I live on my own, have major bills to pay, and I have a daughter. You live with your mom, do not have major bills, and do not have kids. You haven't been through a lot, like I have," Vance explained. That was the most bogus explanation she had ever heard. He did not even want to give her a chance. But he sure did not mind her driving to visit him all the time! Pamela was extremely disappointed, and she let it show.

She absolutely did not agree with him and was upset that she had wasted her time and money on this guy. She was angry that he let this go on all this time, knowing that he did not want to be in a relationship with her.

She got up and said, "I am sorry that you feel that way and it is a shame. You are missing out on a great person." She walked out and drove home. She cried a little at first, but then she smiled. She was not going to let this get her down. She probably just dodged a bullet anyway! When she got home, she went right to her room. She told her mom that she was exhausted and wanted to rest. Right away, she called Mitch to tell him about what happened.

"I told you not to try to be with him," Mitch said.

"I know, I know. I really thought we had something special going on," she said. "It is so embarrassing that I took all that time to visit him and made that bag for him, all for nothing."

Mitch laughed and said, "It is okay. It is *his* loss. You are an amazing woman, and any guy would be lucky to have you!"

Pamela sighed and told him thank you. She still felt crappy.

14 THE SMILE AND THE CRUSH WITH POTENTIAL

Maybe I should have texted or called him back? Pamela wondered nearly two months after she received that text message from Vance. She did not want him to think that she was okay with how their friendship, relationship, or whatever it was, had ended.

Okay, for real this time. I have to focus on me and stop going out of my way for these guys who are not even serious about being with me, she thought. Working helped distract her. She had gotten that internship at the Architectural firm and was doing well there. It took her a little while to socialize at first, but she was trying hard to stay professional. She wanted to show her boss that she was focused on her tasks.

"Pamela, can you please come into my office?" her manager said. Pamela went in and sat down. She was nervous and hoping that they were not letting her go. "You have been doing a great job here and we were wondering if you would like to work here full time, once you graduate next month?"

Pamela smiled from ear-to-ear and tried to stay calm and remained professional. "Yes, of course. I would love that. Thank you so much," she said.

After her hours were complete at work, she clocked out and headed home. She felt so proud of herself. "Real world, here I come!" she screamed with pride. When she arrived home, she told her mom the great news and called Mitch to tell him too.

As Mitch and Pamela were talking, she went onto social media. She saw a post from one of her classmates, Alejandro, from high school. *He is still so handsome!* she thought. She had a flashback and remembered that he was in the same class as she and Axel had been. It was a photo of him and his daughter, and she was holding an award. Pamela told Mitch to give her a minute and commented on the photo. She wrote, *Congratulations to her! She is growing up beautifully and I am glad to see that you are all doing well!*

She got back on the phone and continued her conversation. Mitch and Pamela gossiped for about a half an hour more, then get off the phone. She went to eat dinner and then got ready for bed.

DING. Pamela heard a notification ringing from her laptop.

Hey stranger! How are you doing? Do you still live in Jacksonville? We should meet up!

— Alejandro

Pamela smiled and was excited to hear from him. She looked around on his page and could see how he had been doing well in school, work, parenthood, and life in general. Of course, she had to check the relationship status...single. Yes! She did not want to look desperate, so she tried to wait a couple of days before responding. Usually, she would be scared that the guy would lose interest and move on, but she had to do things differently this time!

Days turned into weeks and Pamela had been so busy with the internship and school that she still had not replied to Alejandro. "Let's go, Hun. We don't want to be late for your graduation!" Sarah shouted from across the house.

"I'm coming, I'm coming!" Pamela shouted back. Pamela quickly went on social media to post a pre-graduation photo of herself in her cap and gown. *I did it!* she captioned under the photo. She grabbed her purse and ran to the door. When they arrived at the ceremony, it was so crowded! It was a lovely thing to see. Pamela felt so proud as she walked through the sea of black gowns and smiling faces. She and her mom made their way to their seats. Her mom was up in the balcony seating and Pamela was in the floor seating with the other graduating students. After about thirty minutes, names were called by department and each student got up to get their diploma. Pamela's program was next and last, so her class had to go backstage to line up.

"Architectural Program. Bachelor of Design," the announcer said. One by one, Pamela and her classmates walked across the stage. As Pamela walked across, she heard her mom screaming her lungs out and cheering. She looked over and saw her mom and her friends standing and waving. Pamela smiled and held a fist up high above her head! Once everyone got back to their seats, the university's president said congratulations and all the students did the hat toss!

"I'm so proud of you!" Sarah said as they walked outside.

"Congratulations, girl! We are proud of you. You worked hard for this!" Mitch said, speaking for him and all her friends.

"You did it, sweetie! I am proud of you," Pamela's dad, Lee, said.

"Thanks for coming all this way for my graduation, Dad!" Pamela said. Her dad lived across country and she rarely got to see him. One by one, her friends came up and gave her hugs.

"Thank you all so much! Let's go eat!" Pamela said.

DING. Pamela got a social media notification on her phone. She looked and saw that it was Alejandro! His message read, *Congratulations Grad! All your hard work has paid off! Let me know if you want to meet up and celebrate this weekend!*

Mitch looked at Pamela and smirked. "Let me guess—that was Alejandro."

Pamela smiled, blushed, and said, "Yes, that was him and he wants to hang out this weekend! This is the second time in a row that he has asked. That is a good sign, right?"

Mitch shook his head while laughing and said, "Here you go again!" The group dispersed and met up at the restaurant. They stayed for an hour or so and then went home.

"I have to get going, sweetie. Congrats again and I am so proud of you. I love you," Lee told Pamela. He gave her a hug and drove off.

When Pamela and Sarah arrived home, they were exhausted. Sarah took a shower and went straight to bed. Pamela did the same, but she could not sleep. She was too hyped up from the day. She looked at her phone and saw a missed text message from Vance. It read, *Hey, congrats on graduating!*

Pamela rolled her eyes. She sent a quick text back that just said, *Thanks*. She did not want to be completely rude by not responding at all, so she just decided to be cold instead. She opened her laptop and realized that she still had not responded to Alejandro! *Crap! I messed up. He probably thinks I'm ignoring him!*

She quickly wrote him back, saying, *Hey Alejandro! Sorry for only just writing you back. Today was hectic! I am doing well and yes, I still live in Jacksonville. I would love to hang out! I really want to go to the beach this weekend though. I need to unwind!* A couple hours went by and she still could not get to sleep. She watched a little TV and started to drift to sleep.

When Pamela woke up the next morning, she saw that Alejandro had written her back. His message read, *I'm glad to hear that! I have not lived in Jacksonville in years. I moved to Daytona Beach. Why don't you just come down here to go the beach, so we can hang out? Here's my number...*

Pamela looked at the clock. She wanted to make sure she did not text him too early in the morning. *He should be up by now,* Pamela thought. She saved his number in her phone and texted him.

Hey Alejandro, this is Pamela. Do you want to meet up later today...maybe around 2 p.m.? Let me know.

Not even ten minutes later, she received a text back. *This is nice. He responds quickly and doesn't leave me hanging. Okay, don't read too much into this though...* she thought.

That sounds great, he texted back. *Yes, that time works for me. You can meet me at my apartment and then we can go to the beach together from there. Here's my address...*

This was going very smoothly. Pamela was

pleasantly surprised, but not surprised at the same time. He seemed to be a great guy with a good head on his shoulders. Yes, she was technically driving there to meet a guy, but she was going to the beach anyway. She wasn't *only* going to see him. So, in her mind, this was not the same.

It took her less than two hours to get to his apartment. She knocked on his door and tried to act cool.

"Hey, beautiful! Glad you made it safely. Come on in," he said, giving her a tight hug.

"Hey, thanks for the invite!" Pamela said. As she walked in, she heard chatter. She had butterflies in her stomach because she did not expect to meet strangers today. There was a small group of people in the living room. Pamela was feeling slightly disappointed, because she thought she and Alejandro were going to hang out alone. He introduced everyone to her as his classmates and roommates and then they left after a few minutes. *Oh okay, they are not coming with us. Whew!* she thought.

Alejandro walked to his room and yelled, "I'll be ready in five minutes. Can we use your car to go to the beach?"

RED FLAG. Pamela silently sighed and said, "Of course. But where is your car?"

He walked into his bathroom and said, "It's in the shop," then returned and added, "Okay, I'm ready. Let's hit the road. The traffic here gets pretty hectic."

They left the apartment and walked to the car. He walked towards the passenger side door to open it.

RED FLAG. *Wow, the least he can do is drive us there*, Pamela thought as she walked toward the driver's side of the car.

"I'll drive, if that's okay," he said while holding the door for her. Pamela smiled and said that it was okay, and she got in the car.

Okay, false alarm. He is a gentleman, she thought.

He got into the driver's seat and noticed the gas tank was about a quarter full. "Looks like your car needs a little gas. There is a gas station up the road," he said. They both buckled their seatbelts and he pulled out of the parking lot. They arrived at the gas station and he got out to pump the gas. As he went in to pay, Pamela smiled. *He is such a gentleman. He just put gas in my car and paid for it. Is this a date?* Alejandro walked back, got in the car, and then drove off. He turned on the radio and then merged onto the interstate.

As they caught up on what had been going on in each other's lives through the years, Pamela could not stop smiling. He held great conversation that was about both of them and he was still hilarious. They reminisced on the fun times in class back in high school and could not stop laughing.

"I'm starving. There's this great place by the beach that I want to take you to."

Pamela smiled and told him that she was hungry too. They pulled up to the Latin café and went in. It was a small, authentic place. You could tell that the food was going to be amazing! Alejandro opened the door for her, and she walked in. The smell of fresh cilantro and seasoned meats made her mouth water. As they waited in line, Pamela tried to figure out if he would pay for lunch. As the line moved, he stayed behind her.

RED FLAG. She tried not to analyze his every move but wondered if he was trying to hint to her that she had to pay for her own lunch, since he had just paid for her gas. Pamela tried to focus on the conversation as the butterflies in her stomach grew.

As Pamela reached the counter, Alejandro walked up and stood next to her and put his order in, then he turned to her and asked her what she would like. As she put her order in, he pulled out his wallet to pay. *Whew*, she thought as she snuck out a silent sigh of relief. *This has to be a date*. While waiting for their food, Alejandro became very flirtatious, and Pamela flirted back. This was going great!

"Number seven!" a woman called.

Alejandro looked down at his receipt and said, "That's us. Let's go." They grabbed the food and went back to the car to grab their towels. They walked to the beach that was just across the street and found a place to sit. Placing the blankets on the sand, they put their food on the blankets. Alejandro took off his shirt and Pamela took off her shirt and shorts to reveal her bikini.

They sat down and started eating, soaking up the sun and breathing in the salty air.

"This food is so amazing!" Pamela said.

"I agree!" Alejandro said.

They ate and talked for about thirty minutes and then Alejandro asked her if she worked out. "I work out from time to time, but nothing too intense," she said.

"Oh yeah? You have an amazing body. But if you had a flat stomach, you'd be perfect!"

HUMUNGOUS RED FLAG!

Pamela felt like she was just punched in the gut. No pun intended. She tried to act as if that comment did not just hurt her feelings. "Yeah, I have been wanting to work on that, but I figured after I have kids, I can work on it then. I don't want to waste my time getting a flat stomach if pregnancy will mess it up anyway," she said.

"You should be able to do it; muscle memory will help you get flat again after you give birth," he told her.

Pamela forced a smile and said, "That's good to know." There was silence for a few minutes, but the crashing of the waves made it less awkward. Alejandro told a few jokes and jump-started a new conversation that made Pamela forget about his comment for a while. To pass the time, they sunbathed, walked along the beach, and searched for shells in the sand. Pamela looked up and noticed that it was starting to look a little overcast.

"I hope it is not going to rain. I still have to drive back home."

Alejandro looked up at the sky. "Yeah, it looks like it may rain. We can go back to my apartment and you can wait it out."

They walked back to their spot and picked up their stuff before heading back to the car. As they drove back to his apartment, it started raining—hard!

"Ugh!" Pamela said.

"Don't worry, if the rain doesn't stop in time, you can crash at my place," he offered. When they arrived at his apartment, he received a phone call. Pamela could not hear the conversation, but could guess what was said, based on his replies. Apparently, his friends wanted to go out tonight. Pamela was too exhausted and did not want to go out. She just wanted to relax and try to get closer to him. They walked through the door and he showed her to the bathroom that was linked to his bedroom.

"There are some fresh towels and soap in the closet if you need them. You can shower in here and I will use the other bathroom," he said. Pamela took a shower and changed into her dry clothes. She walked out of the bathroom and looked around his bedroom. It was clean and smelled so nice. She sat on the bed and watched TV as she waited for him. A few minutes later, he walked in wearing grey sweatpants and a white t-shirt and laid on his bed next to her. He grabbed the remote and found a movie. A comedy, of course.

KNOCK. KNOCK. KNOCK. Midway through the movie, they heard a knock on his bedroom door. Alejandro said they could come in and a few of his roommates and friends came in. They were all dressed up and ready to go out. "Come on, man, are y'all going to get dressed? We're going to the bars tonight!"

Alejandro, clearly somewhat disappointed, told them that he and Pamela were going to stay in. Pamela felt a little bad about not going, but she did not drink and did not want to be the only person not drinking in the group. She knew that she would not have any fun and did not want to go just to please him.

"Are you sure you're okay with not going out?" Pamela asked him.

"Yeah, yeah, it is not a problem at all. We can finish watching the movie." They cuddled and kissed a bit during the movie. Pamela stopped him and told him that she did not want to go too far with him that night, since they were not in a relationship. He was nice about it and they went back to just cuddling and finished watching the movie. Pamela felt guilty that she ruined his night not once, but twice.

"You know what? Let's just go out. Maybe we can catch up with your friends?" Pamela suggested.

Alejandro smiled and said, "Let's do it!" They

both got off the bed and freshened up. They left the apartment and headed downtown. The nightlife was a little slow because it was still early in the evening. Hand-in-hand, they walked up and down the sidewalks. They walked into one of the bars and found a seat.

"Where are your friends?" Pamela asked.

"They've already been to a few bars, so they went to the karaoke bar up the street...anyway, do you drink at all?" Alejandro asked.

"No, I don't drink, and I've never had a drink before," Pamela admitted. She was feeling like she was ruining his night once again. Was one shot *really* that bad?

"What can I get for you guys?" the bartender asked. Alejandro looked over to Pamela and she looked like she wanted to give in.

"What drink do you suggest for a newbie?" Alejandro asked.

"The Candy Shot is a popular one," the bartender said. "I need to see some ID."

Pamela and Alejandro handed over their IDs. The bartender made the shots and placed them down on the counter.

"Bottoms up," he said and swallowed it in one gulp.

Pamela sipped a little of it and pinched her lips.

"It's strong. You have to just throw It back," he told her.

She tried but she could only get it down in two gulps. He asked for another and Pamela shook her head to show the bartender that she did not want any more. Alejandro threw it back in one gulp and pulled her to the dance floor. After an hour of dancing and chugging glasses of water, Pamela grew tired. She was not used to partying like that, so she could not hang out all night.

"Are you getting tired? I thought that shot would have given you a boost!" Alejandro teased.

Pamela smiled and said, "Yeah, I am. I'm sorry. I'm not used to being out all night." She felt bad that he wouldn't be able to have fun with his friends tonight, but at least she made the effort to go out at all.

"That's okay," he said with a smirk.

They left the bar and walked back to the car. Pamela only had one drink and felt fine to drive, but she didn't want to be like Rod and drive under the influence, so she called a cab instead. She just prayed that her car would still be there in the morning and not get towed. They got back to the apartment and she crashed in his bed. He covered her with a blanket and went to sleep on the couch in the living room. Pamela was not asleep, though. She was fighting with herself. There were so many amazing thigs about this guy, but there were some things about him that she just could not accept.

The next morning, Alejandro walked into his room and gently woke her up. "Good morning, beautiful," he said to her.

She smiled and said, "Good morning. What time is it?"

"It is almost eleven," he told her.

"I have to get going." She got up and went into the bathroom. After brushing her teeth, she walked back into the room to grab her stuff. "Thanks for showing me a good time," Pamela told him.

"No problem. I had fun, too," he said. He walked her to the door and told her to have a safe trip home and to let him know when she made it to her house. He hugged her and she walked out the door. She called a cab to drive her back to her car. Thankfully, her car was still there.

She pulled out of the parking lot and merged onto the interstate. While driving home, she replayed the entire trip in her mind. She was disappointed and confused. *Will I ever find the right guy?* She wondered. She knew that there was no such thing as the perfect man, but there must be one who was perfect for *her*. Maybe *it is* me. I need to work on myself first, before trying to be in a relationship with someone else. Once I do that, maybe I will finally meet the right guy.

She had been thinking so much that time flew by! The next thing she knew, she was already home. She texted Alejandro to tell him that she was home and thanked him again for a good time. She was exhausted, so she took the longest nap ever.

15 THE SMILE AND THE FITNESS TRAINER WITH POTENTIAL

Pamela decided to drown her sorrows in ice cream. Or in this case, frozen yogurt. She texted Mitch and asked him if he wanted to meet up and chat.

"So, how was your trip?" Mitch asked Pamela as they walked up to the frozen yogurt place. Pamela shrugged and said it was okay.

As her best friend, Mitch knew there was a long story behind that short answer. "Spill it, girl. What happened?" he asked.

She sighed and told him the story as they moved through the line. They paid for their treats and found a booth in the corner near the window.

"He said that!?" Mitch asked.

"Yeah, and it didn't make me feel good. I thought I was looking cute and in shape and then he dropped that bomb on me," she said.

Mitch shook his head and said, "You are amazing, and you will find the right guy one day. He is going to think that you are perfect just the way you are."

Pamela smiled a little and ate the last scoop of frozen yogurt that was halfway melted in her cup. "Yeah, I guess so. Donnie just told me the same thing." Donnie was one of her friends from the group she'd hung out with in high school.

"You two kept in contact all this time?" Mitch asked.

"Yeah, on and off. Through the years, we would randomly message each other on social media. Nothing major. I would ask him for some fitness advice, and he would send me some of his exercise videos. He is a fitness trainer now." Pamela said as she stood up to throw her trash away. Mitch got up, threw his cup away, and they walked out. Mitch bent down to give Pamela a hug and wished her well. Pamela thanked him then Mitch got into his car and drove home.

Pamela walked to her car and opened the door. As she sat down, she received a notification on her phone. She looked down and saw that it was a message from Donnie. The message read, *Hey Pam, I'm just checking to see how you are doing. Are you feeling better?*

Pamela messaged back and said, *Hey Don, I am okay. Just finished getting some frozen yogurt with my best friend.* She laid her phone down on the passenger seat and drove home. When she arrived, she said goodnight to Sarah and then went straight to her room. She took off her jacket and caught her reflection in the full-length mirror on her wall. She lifted her shirt to reveal her stomach. *Maybe I could tone up a little bit. It is not that big of a deal and it would look nice,* Pamela thought.

She opened her laptop and saw that Donnie was online, so she messaged him. *I think I may actually want to work on my stomach a little. Do you have any workouts that I can do from home that are not too extreme?* she asked.

Sure! I have a couple of workouts that I think you would like, but it would be easier for you to stick with it if we worked out together at the gym. What do you think? Donnie asked. He added his phone number to the following message.

Pamela got off her computer and texted him, *That sounds like a great idea. I can meet you three times a week after I get off work.*

Donnie replied, *Okay, great. Please send me a couple pics of your stomach and let me know what you want to work on.*

Pamela was hesitant but decided to be open and trust him with her insecurity. She sent him a few different views of her stomach and told him that she would like to have more of an hourglass shape and to flatten her stomach a little.

Not a problem! We can get you to where you want to be easily. When would you like to get started? Donnie asked. Pamela told him that she could start the following day.

The first week of her training with Donnie went smoothly. He was so motivating, caring, and made Pamela feel amazing.

"Okay, one more set. Let's go! You can do it!" Donnie said.

Pamela pushed through it and completed her workout. "Thanks again for helping me. I feel great and I'm already starting see a difference!" Pamela said.

Donnie gently placed his hand on her shoulder and said, "No problem. You are doing great!"

Pamela wiped down the machine and they both headed over to the front desk to grab a water. As they walked out, Donnie grabbed Pamela's hand to hold it while he walked her to her car. Pamela felt butterflies in her stomach. She was not expecting to feel this way. When they got to her car, they both did not want to leave, so they started to talk about random things. They talked for hours and the conversation was honest, probing, and interesting. Pamela was learning so much about him and was so glad that she went out of her comfort zone with him.

This is too good to be true. Something is bound

to come up one of these days, Pamela thought.

Donnie looked at his phone. "Woah! It is almost midnight!" he said.

Pamela looked at her phone to verify and smiled. "I cannot believe that we have been talking for this long!" she said. They both stood there awkwardly for a minute or two and giggled. He was trying to make a move and she was waiting for him to make a move. He slowly moved toward her and kissed her. Pamela felt weak in the knees and lightheaded. They both giggled and he told her to drive safe and have a good night. Pamela just smiled and got into her car. As he walked to his car, Pamela stared at him through her review mirror. *Maybe he is the one!* she thought. She finally drove off and replayed the kiss in her head over and over until she made it home.

As Pamela walked in the house, Sarah was up watching TV. She turned it down and asked about Pamela's night. "Ma, this guy is so great. We worked out and then we talked for hours after. We talked about almost everything!"

Sarah smirked and said, "Is that all that happened? He kissed you, didn't he? I know you and you are smiling too hard for just having a good conversation with him."

Pamela smiled big and confessed to the kiss. "Ma, that was the best kiss I have had in my whole life. It was perfect," Sarah said.

"That's because there are real feelings there. I'm happy for you, hun, and I hope this one will work out."

As Pamela walked off, Sarah stopped her. "Hey, I was cleaning out the garage and found this collage of pictures from when you were in high school. I put it in your room, so I wouldn't accidentally toss it out."

Pamela thanked her and went to her room to look. "Ma! Come here and see this!" Pamela shouted from across the house. Sarah rushed over to see what the fuss was about. Pamela held up the collage and pointed to one of the photos. It was of a guy on a school bus. It was the largest photo on the collage and located in the center of the board.

"Who's that?" Sarah asked.

"Ma...that's Donnie!" Pamela exclaimed. "This is the picture that I took of him when we went on our senior field trip to the amusement park back in high school!"

Sarah smiled and said, "Well, isn't that something? You know I don't believe in coincidences. Maybe this was meant to be."

Pamela flipped the board to face her and she stared at the photo with a huge smile. Sarah told Pamela she loved her and went back to her room. Pamela grabbed her phone and took a picture of the collage and sent it to Donnie. *Hey Don, I made it home. Check this out!*

Donnie replied, *I am glad you made it home safely. I did not know you even took that picture of me! That was a fun trip. You have no idea how lucky I felt when you sat next to me that day on the bus!*

Pamela texted back, *goodnight :-)*

Months flew by and Donnie and Pamela grew more serious. He had met her family, but she had not met his yet.

RED FLAG. *Maybe it is difficult for them to travel? They do live across country. Maybe he is not ready yet? Maybe he is not that serious about me, like I thought?* Questions were filling up her mind. Christmas was coming up, so maybe she would meet them then.

"Hey Pamela, we are about to put up the Christmas tree!" Amy said. Pamela jumped and looked up. She was at work and did not realize that she had zoned out.

"Okay, I'm coming." She walked over to the reception area, where everyone was gathered. Amy grabbed a strand of lights and Pamela grabbed some garland. Others grabbed the ornaments. After the tree was complete, everyone stood back to admire their work. The company's owner, Cody, walked behind the tree. He plugged in the lights and everyone clapped.

"Thank you for all of your hard work and happy holidays! Your bonuses are with your managers." Once the bonuses were distributed, some went back to work, and some had to leave work early to travel.

Pamela was one of the ones who stayed in the office to work.

Ready for lunch? Donnie texted her.

Sure. I have to finish an assignment at work first. I will be ready in about fifteen minutes, she texted back. After about twenty minutes or so, she had completed her assignment and gave it to her manager. Donnie was waiting in the parking lot already. She hopped in his car and they drove to her favorite restaurant.

"I have a surprise for you," Donnie said.

"What is it?" Pamela asked.

"You'll see when we get inside," he said vaguely. They walked into the steakhouse and someone waved at Donnie to show him where they were seated. There was his family sitting at the table! His mom, dad, sister, and older brother. Everyone introduced themselves to Pamela, one by one, and his mom got up and gave Pamela a tight hug.

"It is so nice to meet all of you!" Pamela said. "I was wondering when I would get to meet you guys. I was starting to get a little worried," she added as she giggled.

"He is always talking about you and he has been planning this gathering for months! It was simply hard to get all of our schedules together, so we could all meet you at the same time."

Pamela looked at Donnie and smiled. *I guess that was a false red flag that I had not met his family yet...whew!* Pamela thought.

Halfway into the meal, a group of waitresses and waiters gathered around the booth and shouted, "Surprise!". They brought over slices of cake, balloons, and a small gift box.

"What's going on? Is it someone's birthday?" Pamela asked.

"Which one of you is Pamela?" one of the waitresses asked.

Pamela raised her hand. "That's me," she said softly. The waitress grabbed the gift box and handed it to her. The group clapped and cheered. Pamela opened it and it was a beautiful Pandora beaded charm bracelet. She was in tears. She got up and gave Donnie a hug and a kiss. *This truly may be the real thing!* she thought.

The next hour and a half brought so much laughter and joy. His mom and dad told funny childhood stories about all the kids and about how adventurous and hilarious Donnie was as a child.

"Can I get anything else for you all?" their waitress asked.

"No, we are fine. Thank you for everything," Donnie said. His dad paid for the meal and everyone headed to their cars. They all said goodbye to each other and gave Pamela hugs.

"Your family is so sweet and cool!" Pamela told Donnie.

"They really like you; I can tell," he told her.

"Thank you for my bracelet. It is so my style," she said. Donnie hugged her and held her hand as they walked to his car. He dropped her off back at her job, and she completed her day, while he went to spend quality time with his family.

Christmas came and went. Donnie traveled with his family back to his hometown to spend the winter break with them. Pamela stayed home with her mom.

"Have you heard from Donnie lately?" Sarah asked.

"No. He is back in Pennsylvania with his family. Maybe he has just been busy with them," Pamela said. She texted him a couple times and called him once with no response.

RED FLAG. *I hope he is okay,* Pamela thought. She went into her room and opened her laptop. She tried to look on social media to see if he had posted anything. No posts. Another week went by and Pamela grew more worried by the day. Was he ignoring her? Did something happen to him? So many thoughts went through her mind. She did not know what to believe. She just hoped that this was not another repeat of the situation with Rod! Things were going so well with her and Donnie and she would be devastated if he ghosted her now!

BING. Pamela received a text from Donnie. The messaged read, *Hey Pamela, I am so sorry that you haven't heard from me. My family and I went on a camping trip and got snowed into the cabin! We were just recused this morning! I will give you a call once we are back home. Love, Donnie*

This was a wild story and Pamela was trying to believe it but was hesitant. *Really? He really thinks that I am going to believe this?* Pamela thought. She walked to her mom's room to get her opinion on the situation. "I finally heard from Donnie. He just told me that he and his family were snowed in and trapped in their cabin this whole time. I guess this was the best story that he could come up with?" Pamela said with an attitude.

"Umm...honey, have you been watching the news at all? There was a huge snowstorm that hit, and Pennsylvania got hit hard. There were several stories of people getting snowed in. He told you the truth."

Pamela breathed a sigh of relief and said, "Oh. Thank goodness. I really thought he was blowing me off this whole time."

Sarah smiled and said, "Hun, I know you have been through a lot with guys through the years, but Donnie is a good one. You have to try to trust him unless he truly gives you a reason not to."

"You're right," Pamela said. She walked back into her room. Her stomach was in knots and she felt such guilt. While she was being negative and losing faith in him, he was in a terrible situation that could have

180

ended badly. She was suddenly overwhelmed with love for him and was so glad that she did not confront him about not responding to her. She could not wait for him to call, so she could tell him how she truly felt. *Another false red flag...whew!* Pamela thought. Pamela waited all day for Donnie to call her. She did not want to call him because she wanted to give him space to recover and take care of things.

RING. RING. RING.

"Hello?" Pamela answered.

"Hey, it's Donnie. We finally made it back home," he replied.

"I am so happy that you all are safe. I have to tell you some—"

Donnie interrupted her. "Wait. Before you say anything else. I have to confess..." Pamela had butterflies in her stomach and was thinking this was it; he was about to dump her after all. "I love you, Pamela. I already had strong feelings for you, but this trip really made me realize that I need you in my life."

KNOCK. KNOCK. KNOCK.

"Pamela! Can you get the door please!?" Sarah said.

"Hold on a sec. Someone is at the door," Pamela told Donnie. She walked out of her room, through the hallway and to the door. She reached to unlock the door and opened it.

"SURPRISE!"

To her surprise, she saw a crowd of people. It was his friends, her friends, and both of their families standing outside. Even her dad was there! They were all standing behind Donnie and holding sparklers. Pamela looked down and saw Donnie bent on one knee, holding a small black velvet box. Pamela began to tear up and started giggling.

Sarah walked behind Pamela and whispered, "I told you to trust him." Sarah led Pamela closer to Donnie, hugged her and joined the rest of the group.

Donnie slowly opened the box and revealed a beautiful ring. He gently grabbed her trembling left hand and said, "As I was saying…I need you in my life and I love you so much. Will you do me the honor of becoming my wife?"

Without hesitation, Pamela screamed, "YES, YES, YES! I will!"

As the crowd cheered, someone shot off fireworks in the background and lit up the sky. Pamela jumped into his arms and they kissed passionately. They stared into each other's eyes and Pamela could not stop smiling. Permanent smile achieved.

ABOUT THE AUTHOR

K.R. Denson is a mother of two, a shoemaker, owner of K2L Customs LLC. and now… an author! She graduated from the University of Florida in 2010 with a bachelor's degree in Interior Design and landed a job as a Design Consultant at an office furniture dealership. She started the job months before graduating and worked there for over 9.5 years. In 2019, with the support of her husband, she made the decision to stay home full time to focus on her growing family and starting her own business. At the beginning of the Covid-19 pandemic lockdowns in 2020, she explored several artistic avenues to keep her peace of mind. After taking writing classes and brainstorming several book ideas, she took a chance and wrote her first young adult novella. She wrote this story to show young adults that they are not alone in the awkward world of dating and that faith, patience and staying true to yourself will lead you to "the one".

Made in the USA
Las Vegas, NV
31 May 2021